ONE SNOWY NIGHT

Ellen Moore

A KISMET™ Romance

METEOR PUBLISHING CORPORATION
Bensalem, Pennsylvania

A special thanks to:

Kate, Peggy and "the Reader" for the chance.

Marylee and Joan for trudging through every trench with me.

The truckers of the world for the inspiration.

Tom for the romance.

And God for all the above.

ELLEN MOORE

After having moved six times in ten years, Ellen Moore has learned never to say, "This is the last time we're moving." (She's collected some great background info for future books, however). Right now, she and husband, Tom, live in Georgia with three large tanks of tropical fish. In her "spare time," she likes to read, fish, and make crafts.

ONE

"Breaker one–nine. Breaker one–nine. This is the Lone Star. Dixie Darlin', you got your ears on?"

The crackle of static in the CB radio preceded a lush, feminine voice as intoxicating as a long swig of Southern Comfort. "This is Dixie Darlin' coming back at you, Lone Star."

"Well, Darlin', what are you up to this fine afternoon?"

"Up to my Dixie Darlin's in snow and sleet, that's what!"

Randy Taylor, known as Lone Star to his trucking buddies, let out a low growl. "Sounds mighty erotic to me."

Dixie's tone flattened. "Star, *you* are a sick puppy."

Her rebuke curved Randy's lips into a smile that produced a long furrow in each of his shallow cheeks. He liked this good-natured taunting from her. It made him feel like a younger brother—someone special, although he knew Dixie would never admit it.

"What can I say? That's just the kind of guy I am."

"That's what I hear." Dixie sighed. "Good Lord, are we in the Klondikes instead of coastal North Carolina? It doesn't snow like this in Carolina this time of year."

"Yeah, but ain't it pretty?" Randy drawled, laying on a thick icing of his Texas accent.

7

"Star, have you been driving with your head hanging out the window?! Your brain's frostbit if you think this is pretty. It's treacherous, boy! *I'm* praying I make it to Charleston in one piece, and *you're* admiring the countryside as if it was a Currier and Ives Christmas card!"

As Dixie scolded him for his apparent lack of concern over the uncharacteristic snowstorm, Randy cast an uncertain glance out his side window. His reservations about the driving conditions matched Dixie's—maybe even surpassed hers. His high spirits had nothing to do with the weather, however.

"Wait a minute." Dixie interrupted his chastisement. "Is that jubilation of yours a direct result of owning a brand-new rig?"

Randy checked his watch. Eleven after four. He'd figured it would take her five minutes to guess he owned the vehicle of his dreams. It took her only three.

"Yup. I picked it up in Greensboro about lunch time."

The long blast of Dixie's horn told Randy she shared his excitement.

That didn't surprise him since Dixie knew more about his personal business than the women he kept company with on an intimate basis. Although he and Dixie had never laid eyes on each other, they managed to maintain a two-year friendship linked together only by the CB. Their schedules might one day coincide so they could have a beer together at some truck stop, but for now, this was just fine. There was something comforting about confiding in a woman when he couldn't look her in the eye. He opened up to Dixie about things he'd tell no one else.

That Georgia peach voice could belong to a Spanish onion for all he cared. Dixie was his friend. She shared his interest in trucking. He'd saved every penny he could spare for the last five years to buy this metallic blue and chrome Peterbilt, and he could think of no one better to share his pleasure with.

"How does it handle, Star?"

"Like an expensive woman, Darlin'. Like an expensive woman."

"And how would *you* know about expensive women?"

The rebuttal forming on Randy's tongue slipped back down his throat as the butter-colored beams of his headlights snagged a movement along the side of the road up ahead. Instinct triggered him to slow down, even though he'd been crawling for the last hour. Every trucker in this territory knew a movement could mean a deer and a deer could spell disaster if it leapt before a semi.

A few more rolls of the wheels and Randy could see that the life form stood erect and struggled to remain that way in the wind and snow, but it *was* human.

A person on this deserted slice of 211-A just didn't make sense.

This was Randy's home stretch. He knew every pebble in the asphalt strip like he knew every lump in his own bed. Nothing, not even an abandoned barn, stood to offer shelter. He hadn't encountered another vehicle, disabled or otherwise, for miles. He couldn't imagine someone so uncaring they would discard a hitchhiker on a night like this.

So, did the person drop from the sky with the snow?

"Hey! Star! Did I hurt your feelings?"

"Wh–?" Randy's thoughts snapped back to Dixie and he said, "No . . . I just got me a little development up ahead."

"What kind of development?"

"A hitchhiker."

"On a night like this?! Is he an idiot?"

"Probably some teenager who's run away from home because his parents wouldn't let him borrow the car tonight." Randy's clear voice filmed with disdain. Of course, to him, teenagers and idiots were one in the same. He couldn't help it—he was not fond of today's youth. These days, the trend was laziness, disrespect, and poor attitude. Adolescents were aliens he couldn't understand no matter how hard he tried.

"Well, don't be too hard on the fool, Star," Dixie said and reminded him, "It's not been so long ago *you* were one yourself."

Randy wondered if Dixie's "one" meant a fool or a teenager. He could have informed her he wasn't spoiled, nor did he have parents to worry half to death when he was young. But then, Dixie didn't have to know everything about him.

Shifting to a lower gear, he mentally measured the distance so he could stop somewhere near the kid.

"I'll try to refrain from beating him to death before I return him to his parents, Dixie."

"You can fill me in on the details when I get back from Charleston . . . If I make it back, that is."

Randy had no doubts Dixie could handle any disaster— natural or manmade. "You keep it between the ditches."

"You do the same," Dixie told him before she ten-foured and signed-off.

Bringing the semi to a halt on the ice-coated asphalt proved to be trickier than he thought it would be. Satisfaction sparkled in his eyes as he swung open the passenger door and found himself in perfect alignment with the pedestrian.

"Howdy," Randy greeted the heavily bundled figure who worked so hard for every breath. "Want a ride?"

Independent movements of the person's head and limbs were an impossibility since he wore at least one sample of every winter garment known to man. He twisted his entire body to peer inside the cab.

Until this point, Randy assumed he was offering a lift to an adolescent male. But if those almond-shaped eyes framed in the space between stocking cap and scarf belonged to a member of his own sex, the dude could go it on foot!

Once in a lifetime, Randy'd seen that exact shade of

green—in a ring on a rich lady's finger. A rare jade, he remembered someone saying. Now, two perfect replicas of that stone, fringed by dark blonde lashes, gazed up at him.

Without a word, the girl tossed her two shoulder bags onto the floor and attempted to hoist herself into the truck.

"Grab that bar beside the door," Randy coached her.

She did as he said, but it was of little help. She grunted and huffed and managed to pull herself to the first step.

Randy's patience thinned in the frigid air. He stretched half his five-foot-eleven frame across the cab, grabbed her hands and towed her into the truck, like a fisherman landing a citation tuna.

"Damn!" he exclaimed, breathless from the feat and amazed at her weight. Not only did he have a female teenager on his hands, but a pudgy one, at that. There was no way she could blame the excess pounds on her extra clothing.

He watched in silent wonder as she took another eternity to situate herself on the seat, strap herself in, and close the door a millisecond before they freeze-dried.

Spastic, too. He shook his head.

"Are we ready now?" Randy asked. Though he smiled, his voice contained a fair amount of sarcasm which went right over her head.

She nodded.

Once on the road they traveled in silence. When the cab returned to a reasonable level of warmth, the girl began to unwrap her scarf like a nurse removing a bandage.

Randy glanced at her, then turned again for a good gander.

A yard of strawberry-blonde hair spilled over her shoulders when she yanked the cap off and shook her head. Leaning back against the seat, she looked at him from beneath golden bangs fringing her highly arched brows.

Plump or not, her face was striking. Kind of Meryl

Streep-ish, it had a quality that made a man sit up and take notice, which was exactly what Randy was doing right now.

He remembered the driving conditions and watched the road for a moment before his eyes returned to her. Even in the afternoon light dulled by the overcast sky, he could see a generous helping of freckles spattered across her petite, straight nose and porcelain cheeks. Her lips were so flawless they appeared designed by an expert engineer and not a quirk of nature, and reminded him of cherries. If he took a taste of them, would he be rewarded with his favorite flavor?

"Thank you," she said.

Her husky voice did nothing to force his attention to the road and away from her rich mouth.

Her head lifted in curiosity.

That jerked Randy's eyes back to the road. Couldn't have her thinking he was some pervert riding the roads in search of young women. "My name's Randy Taylor."

"I'm Scarlett."

He grinned at her. "As in O'Hara?"

"As in Kincaid." Horror flared in her eyes for a split second before she shielded it.

Randy, acting as if he'd not noticed her fear, quickly faced the road. "Well, Scarlett Kincaid, where are you headed?"

"Where are you going?"

One look and he knew she was serious. She didn't care where she went.

"I live in a small town called Dominion about an hour from here," Randy said. "That's where I'm headed."

Scarlett shifted on the seat and grimaced.

"You all right?" he asked.

She nodded. "They sure don't make these things for the comfort of the passenger, do they?"

Randy grinned. "I wouldn't know. I've never ridden on the passenger side."

"Well, it's better than walking," she said absentmindedly and stared out the window. "This Dominion a big city?"

Randy laughed out loud. "If there was a trailer on this rig, you could put all of Dominion's citizens in it and they'd still have room for company. The town caters to truckers. Only a small population calls it home."

Scarlett rested her head against the seat again. "Dominion is fine. I'll hitch a ride from there."

"I doubt you will tonight," Randy told her. "The only people who might be moving are the truckers, but they'd just as soon park for the night and have a few cold ones at Preston's Bar and Grill. They don't care to drive another hour to Wilmington in weather like this. And the good citizens wouldn't dare leave *their* warm living rooms."

Scarlett focused on the steady pummeling of sleet upon the windshield and said nothing.

Moments passed and Randy probed, "Mind if I ask you why you were out there tonight?"

"You can ask." Her eyes, two impassive jade orbs in the dim light, swept to him.

Randy could take a hint. One so blatant, anyway. He could ask, but she wouldn't answer. Well, she didn't want to talk about her personal affairs. He could respect that. She left him to form his own theories of why she chose tonight of all nights to wander the countryside. His imagination took flight. For a few minutes she was everything from a spy to a murderess.

At least he could ditch the unhappy-adolescent-trying-to-escape-tyrannical-parents concept.

How old is she, anyway?

His blue eyes slid to the right in a sneaky sideways glance. He couldn't be more than four or five years older than her, which made her at least twenty-four—more like twenty-five.

Good.

Once in Dominion, he'd drop her off with an adios and

no guilt. She was old enough to take care of herself. It wasn't up to him to suddenly become her keeper.

Satisfied his drive home might be more peaceful than he first suspected, Randy asked, "Mind if I listen to some music?" It didn't matter if she did. He owned the vehicle, but he thought he'd be polite anyway.

Scarlett shook her head and settled onto the seat wearily.

As Randy reached for the radio knob, he wondered how long she'd trudged through the elements before he happened to come along. She looked pretty tuckered.

Waylon Jennings's latest hit echoed through the truck and Randy concentrated on his driving. A country music classic followed Waylon's closing note. A third melody trailed it. By the time the fourth song began to play, Randy could take no more.

The flair for conversation was as much a part of him as the blue of his eyes and the curl of his brown hair. As a country boy and a Texan, if he couldn't make this lady converse with him, he might as well hang up his boots and Stetson.

"So, are you from around these parts?" he asked.

"No."

"Neither am I," he admitted. "I'm a transplant from Texas. I moved here about four years ago. I like the people . . ."

Randy glanced at Scarlett. She was watching the meadows as they passed by, their blurry images reminiscent of a child's snow globe just tilted and shaken.

Is she listening?

"So, I bet you're asking yourself how a guy like me could end up in a hole-in-the-wall like Dominion."

She shot him a don't-bet-your-next-paycheck-on-it look.

Yup. She's listening.

"That's exactly what I asked myself . . . once. I was working for this trucking firm out of Houston, you see. When they decided to open up a branch in Wilmington and send *me* . . . Well, I wasn't too keen on the idea. But I was one of their top drivers so they naturally sent me here. Well, I got lost th—''

"Uh–oh.''

Randy's eyes left the road, thinking Scarlett's comment related to his story. He realized as soon as he looked at her that she probably hadn't heard a word he said. She'd pulled up in her seat, her back a rigid line against the upholstery. Her expression hovered somewhere between astonishment and anguish.

"Uh–oh?''

She nodded. "Uh–oh.''

"What's uh–oh?''

"My water broke.''

She looked at him for a reaction. Her almond-shaped eyes now resembled huge green grapes.

"What water?'' Randy grinned. He was beginning to believe Scarlett *was* an extraterrestrial creature who'd dropped from the sky.

Scarlett's jaw clenched. Her eyes thinned to emerald slashes across her bright crimson face. Hands flying wildly, she unsnapped the seatbelt and fumbled with the buttons of her coat.

Randy alternated glances at the road with quick glimpses at Scarlett. Whatever this series of flamboyant movements produced, he couldn't wait to see it.

Scarlett's black coat parted.

Randy's eyes collided with her generous belly.

She planted a hand on each side of her balloon-shaped stomach and announced, breathlessly, "*This* water, you idiot.''

"You're pregnant.'' Randy's eyes darted to hers. "You're considerably pregnant.'' His smile did a backflip.

"Bingo!'' Scarlett tapped her index finger to her nose as if Randy just guessed the answer in a game of charades.

Her head snapped back in pain. "Ah! In labor would be a better description."

Randy's gaze plunged to the seat. A damp, stain-threatening spot glared back at him. The last of his humor trickled from his face and eyes. "On my new truck seat?" His voice was soft with confusion and disappointment.

Scarlett zeroed-in on him, a vee of disbelief forming between her palomino brows.

"On . . . my . . . new . . . truck . . . seat!" Starting low, Randy's voice built to a crescendo with the final word capable of shattering his new truck windows.

"Yes! Yes! On your new truck seat!" Scarlett retaliated.

"I don't believe this!" Randy slapped his hand on the dash, instead of connecting it with the delicate curve of her cheek. "I haven't had this truck for five hours and now the seat is ruined!"

Scarlett's once kissable mouth twisted in sarcasm. "I'm so sorry. How rude of me not to cross my legs and hold the baby in until we got to a more acceptable location!"

"You could have said something!" Randy shoved a stray swath of nutmeg curls from his forehead as his angry gaze scathed her.

"If I had known, I would have."

"You can't tell me you didn't have *some* indication!" he replied with heavy sarcasm.

Scarlett crossed her arms over her stomach and tilted her head. "Have you ever been pregnant?"

"No." Randy looked away, trying to at least remove her from his sight. He was fantasizing that his fingers were squeezing her fragile neck instead of the steering wheel.

"Neither have I."

Randy eyed her, baffled. She actually found some logic in that statement.

Sensing his bewilderment, Scarlett lifted her chin and turned the tables on him. "I can't believe *you* were so stupid you couldn't guess."

"How am I supposed to know these things?" He took offense. "I'm a confirmed bachelor. And I can't remember ever so much as holding a baby. Besides," he turned to the window and mumbled, "I just thought you were fat."

"Pardon?"

"Nothing."

"You said you thought I was fat!"

God, this woman irked the hell out of him!

"If you knew what I said, then why did you ask me to repeat it?" he barked.

The echo of Randy's voice died in the small space surrounding them and they fell silent. Randy was the first to look away, using safe driving as an excuse. The truth was, he didn't like the emotions swirling within him.

Anger and irritation were at the top of the list, but Scarlett brought out some other feelings he found odd to be experiencing at this particular time. Attraction was the most perplexing of them all. That wealth of blonde hair, those freckles, those lips—most of all, those jade eyes with their infinite gamut of expressions capable of flaring all at one time—all made a pretty picture he couldn't resist enjoying. If she'd just keep her mouth shut.

"Let me out." Scarlett's voice was low and weird in its sudden calm.

"What?" Randy looked at her again, all his gentle feelings dying. "You are an imbecile, lady!"

"So, *now* I'm a fat imbecile!" Scarlett shrieked.

Randy shook his head, not bothering to comment. He focused on the road ahead of him, wishing Scarlett *had* been a runaway kid. In fact, a juvenile delinquent looked mighty good right now. Randy could have bought a kid a meal, listened to his troubles, and made up some horrible stories of life as a runaway to scare the teen back into the arms of his frantic parents. That, Randy could deal with. This pregnant package of trouble was more than he cared to handle.

Was there a mental institution within a fifty-mile radius?

It would be worth the detour. If Scarlett hadn't escaped from a padded room, she sure needed to take up residence in one.

"I want to get out," she repeated, her tone scalpel-sharp.

Randy chuckled and shook his head.

Scarlett heaved air into her lungs and squared her shoulders. "You're not taking me seriously. I am not crazy."

"You could have fooled me," Randy countered as he met her eyes. "There's not a living soul for the next twenty miles. Yet, *you* want to hike it in a snowstorm while you're in labor. Or maybe you just want to have your baby right here. Either way, that spells crazy to me."

Scarlett's mouth clamped tightly over her rebuttal. For some reason known only to God, she decided to be silent.

Good. Randy wanted that.

Scarlett glared at him. Then she glared at the road. Then her expression twisted into one of horror as she screamed loud enough for someone twenty miles away to hear her.

In the split second it took to focus on the highway, Randy imagined Scarlett's terror resulted from a hundred things. Another contraction. A deer in their path. A stalled vehicle . . . Anything, but what he saw. "Oh, damn!"

Before Randy could react, the semi collided with a freak snowdrift which had collected on the highway. Freak? Everything about this afternoon had been *freaky*.

Something snagged the right bumper of the semi as it burst through the snowdrift's core. The Peterbilt twirled 180 degrees, then skidded down the right side of the road. The dizzying kaleidoscope of passing scenery, combined with the dangerous situation disoriented Randy.

As if in a slow-motion replay, they seemed to whirl forever. Everything registered in vivid clarity and detail all at once. The headlights created neon spirals in the snow-speckled twilight like sparklers writing in the dark. The tires skimmed across the slick asphalt with a vibration so slight Randy might not have noticed it under different circumstances. Right now, every nerve in his body felt so magnified that he understood what the fairy-tale princess with a pea beneath her mattress had experienced.

Randy's senses worked overtime. That is, all except his hearing. An eerie quiet filled the cab as the truck skidded across the road. It was as if a soundproof cocoon enveloped him, eliminating the screech of tires and groan of metal.

Silence. Void. Nothing.

He'd never heard such a silence. This was a vacuum; a snowy, icy hole in the universe.

Randy didn't like it at all. It filled him with a panic like he'd never known.

In a futile rush of action, Randy gripped the steering wheel so tight his knuckles blanched. He could feel the tires clutching at the road like a cat attempting to sink its claws into glass. He knew better than to try controlling the gas and brake pedals. Anything he did would jeopardize their situation instead of help it.

The spinning evolved into a cockeyed skid across the center line and the truck moved into the left lane, continuing to skim along the shimmering asphalt.

Randy used the reprieve from centrifugal force to heave air into his starved lungs. Swiping at the tributary of sweat gushing down between his bunched brows, he glanced at Scarlett.

"Fasten your seatbelt!" Randy ordered, swearing that if they lived through this, baby or no baby, he was going to throttle the woman.

Scarlett pried her hands from the seat and obeyed Randy in a horrified silence that gave him a moment's satisfaction.

Randy looked ahead of him, squinting to find his bearings in the storm, which now looked more like someone ripped open a bag of flour. A geyser of curses befitting a seasoned merchant marine spewed from his mouth when he caught a glimpse of what was in store for them.

A meadow.

A knobby, washboard-rough field. *That* concerned him. But the ditch—a two-foot deep gash in the flesh of the frozen earth they had to cross before they reached the field—*petrified* him. With no traction and out of control like this, if the truck rolled over only once, Randy would consider them lucky.

Things were happening too fast for him to consider his options, or to draw from his eleven years of trucking experience. Quite frankly, he really didn't know what to do. He'd never faced something like this before and his mind was numb at the moment. He operated on pure instinct.

If he maneuvered the truck's nose toward the ditch, perhaps it would run right over the gap.

Or the rig could flip onto its back like a dying bug.

Well, Randy had no choice. He wasn't about to let this happen without a fight.

This wasn't *supposed* to be happening, dammit! He was only twenty-nine years old!

But here he was—about to take a trip to that big weigh station in the sky.

That thought made Randy tighten his hold on the steering wheel. He wasn't ready to hand in his manifest of life just yet.

Muscles tensed, heart pounding between his tonsils, Randy stared out the windshield, not that he could see much for sweat sluicing into his eyes. Even with snow outside, he perspired as if this were an August afternoon at the ballpark!

Adrenalin.

At least he *hoped* adrenalin caused the unseasonal sweating, and not the fact that he'd bypassed the whole trial with the big boss upstairs and was heading straight for the jaws of—

The wheels made contact with the ditch—not in perfect alignment, but perhaps enough to keep the truck upright. Nothing more to do, Randy prepared to see what he now considered a brief lifetime flash before his eyes.

As if popping a cork on a bottle of champagne, his ears cleared, allowing him to hear all the sickening sounds he'd been spared until now. Scrunching, screeching . . . screaming.

Somewhere in the maelstrom, the truck screamed an ear-deafening plea for its life.

TWO

"Well, now I think *my* water broke." Randy shook his head to recharge his senses. He opened his eyes, expecting to see the flames of hell lapping at his feet.

The discovery of cold, earthly sleet splattering the windshield was a temporary relief as he saw the unnatural slant of the truck's headlights. A major problem. That acrobatic leap over the ditch, followed by a jolting tiptoe across the frozen ex-tobacco field, was more suitable for a circus act than a ten-wheeler. Disheartened, Randy just knew something real important snapped during impact.

His eyes, now white-hot with fury, seared a path to the woman. Things were fine before he had picked her up. Now look at them.

The corrosive expletive forming on his tongue dissolved like bad medicine when he saw her in the dim light of the dashboard.

Scarlett's pasty complexion reflected the eerie green of the indicator lights—or their "joy-ride" could have caused her peculiar coloring.

Emerald spots of perspiration glistened on Scarlett's forehead and upper lip. Her eyes, fixed upon something only she could see, were wild and wide and dark as damp moss.

She was scared to death.

Well, hell, so was he!

This wasn't a Sunday afternoon drive through the country for him, either. Stranded on one of the most desolate roads in the Wilmington area. His truck probably totalled. Damned near killed by a freak snowdrift!

Randy looked down at himself, suddenly overcome with the need to inventory his vital parts. His heart nearly beat out of his chest. Good! At least it was pumping. His lungs heaved in air like an industrial-sized vacuum cleaner. They were doing their job, too.

The severe landing had slam-dunked him down onto the seat. The seatbelt jerked up to his pectorals, dragging his navy sweatshirt with it.

Randy shoved the shirt down and rearranged himself to a more dignified position. Everything accounted for and in working order, he breathed easier.

An unsteady hand pushed through his hair from his temple to the collar of his shirt and he joined Scarlett in staring straight ahead. It seemed appropriate to meditate after a near-death experience, he supposed.

Beneath their heavy breathing, Randy thought he caught the crooning of America's top country music star. The damned radio continued to play, although the engine conked out at the first sign of trouble! He and Scarlett were stranded, but they could listen to music, by God!

Randy looked at Scarlett. The last time he'd been "entertained" in a vehicle by a heavy-breathing female, it was a much more pleasurable experience.

"Well, are you hurt?" He winced at the concern missing from his voice. Yes, he'd almost met his maker and the truck might only make it to the junk pile, but Scarlett's condition was delicate. He could at least show some compassion.

Scarlett blessed him with a hostile stare, but her eyes were filmed with tears and her voice quivered. "Thanks for your concern."

He deserved that. He felt like a heel.

"Look, I don't want to argue with you. This has gotten way out of hand. All I want to do is get back on the road and drop you off as soon as I can." He reached for the key to see if the truck might have one last breath of life in it. "You've been nothing but trouble since I stopped for you."

She glared at him. "So, you blame me for everything!"

Randy's eyes closed as he fought his frustrations. He couldn't revive the truck, they were stranded miles from civilization, and everything Scarlett did or said annoyed the hell out of him!

One look at her replaced his frustration with anger. It boiled, it bubbled, it erupted to the surface again, and he lost all of his control. "Of course, I think you're to blame! You distracted me."

"I did not distract you."

"You most certainly did. You distracted me with those contractions and talk about getting out of the truck. This would never have happened if you hadn't taken my mind off my driving. I'm a good driver."

"Oh, I can see that," Scarlett returned with a fair amount of sarcasm.

"Look, I don't need your sarcasm right now. This is a real mess we're in, if you haven't noticed. And if you can't say anything to help, then just don't say anything."

Scarlett's lips pressed together, the bottom one itching to poke out like a pouting child. She kept it in check, though. Shaking hands popped open the seatbelt and gathered her belongings.

Randy watched in amazement as Scarlett slid and rolled and flopped around until she tumbled out of the truck—right into a fluffy snowdrift. Teeth gritted, she stepped out of the mound, swayed a bit, and shoved all her weight against the door. It thudded a loud farewell, resounding through the cab, which felt rather empty now.

Randy's eyes leveled in irritation as Scarlett appeared

in the triangle of light at the front of his truck. With her bags draped over her and nine months of baby in her belly, her walk resembled that of a young pachyderm.

Her step faltered. She wrapped her arms about her middle and leaned back in pain. Even from the truck, Randy could see her body tremble.

He forced himself to look away. Scarlett was leaving! He was rid of her and nothing was going to spoil this moment!

Except his eyes. They had a mind of their own and switched back to Scarlett. The contraction over, she now trudged forth with the determination of a soldier seizing enemy territory.

One end of Randy's mouth tipped upward in a smile despite himself. She sure was a stubborn little cuss . . . And probably confused and frightened, he suddenly realized. People that stubborn were usually terrified.

How would he act if he were in her shoes—alone, traveling in a snowstorm on foot, and about to give birth? The latter he couldn't even begin to imagine. The former he knew about all too well. It was scary. He supposed he'd act the same way.

No matter how much she got under his skin and no matter how much he thought she distracted him, they were the only two people for miles. They needed each other. She needed him because she was going to have a baby and he needed her . . . Well, he was sure there was a reason.

Rolling his eyes, Randy reached for the door handle and admonished himself aloud, "Taylor, you're as much out of your mind as she is!"

Scarlett glanced over her shoulder when the door slammed. Her waddle quickened, but Randy's one step equaled two of hers and he closed the distance between them with ease. A few long, lanky strides enabled him to lay a hand upon her shoulder, which she fiercely shrugged off.

Randy's fingers corded about the soft flesh of Scarlett's upper arm. Even through the layers of clothing he could feel the slenderness of her limb and kept its fragility in mind as he forced her to face him.

"Scarlett, what are you doing?" His voice was resigned.

"Trying to get as far away from you and your precious truck as I can!"

He fought the rising urge to assist her, but he'd made his decision to come after her and he'd stick to it. "Well, you won't succeed at this pace. Look, you're not even ten yards from the truck."

As Randy pointed toward the vehicle, the full extent of their good fortune registered and he inhaled a ragged breath. The truck should have been a mangled mass of metal. Except for leaning on its side like a wounded animal and being buried axle deep in the dirt-and-snow quagmire, it remained intact. The rig could have internal damage, but Randy and Scarlett had walked away without a scratch. That said a lot for Peterbilt or perhaps it just wasn't his and Scarlett's time to die. Randy felt a little queasy as he considered what might have happened.

He swallowed and raked both hands through his hair. "Aw, man, look at that."

Randy met Scarlett's eyes. She'd misinterpreted his reaction. Lips compressed, eyes ablaze with fuming determination, she whirled about and walked clumsily away from him.

Stunned, Randy watched her for a moment, allowing her to place a fair amount of distance between them. It took a good trot and some modified wrestling moves to stop her this time.

"Stop doing that!" he ordered. As she twisted in his arms, he could hear her labored breathing and tiny grunts of pain. "Calm down, Scarlett."

"Did you see my thumb stuck out?" she called over her shoulder, still fighting his restraint. "*You* were the one who stopped. I didn't ask for help! You could have just driven right on by.''

He could have. He should have. He'd probably damn himself until his dying day that he didn't do just that. But it wasn't in him to let anyone—even an insane, trouble-making, mother-to-be—die in the frigid wilderness.

"No," he said near her ear, "I couldn't have done that."

Scarlett stilled for a brief moment and Randy released her. She whirled around and her appraising eyes searched his face for a long time.

She looked much like the teenager Randy mistook her for in the first place. Young, vulnerable, suspicious.

He wanted to ask her questions. Mostly he wanted to know what happened to make her so defensive and hostile. Before he could voice his thoughts, a harsh wind rushed over them, reminding Randy of his coatless body and he urged, "Let's get back into the truck. It's freezing out here.''

''I don't want to ruin your truck.''

''Do you think there's anything left to ruin? Look at it.''

Neither of them turned toward the rig, knowing the sight would add fuel to the flames of their argument.

''Think about your baby.'' He appealed to the maternal instinct as a final argument.

Scarlett's eyes lowered and she studied his snow-covered boots. She said nothing.

Randy's stomach churned with dread. He'd experienced firsthand a woman who didn't want her baby. Was he seeing the same situation here?

Randy didn't want children, took every precaution against it. But if an accident happened, he'd never deny his child. He hated those who did.

''Scarlett, you . . . *do* . . . want your baby, don't you?''

Scarlett's head shot up. Her eyes stabbed at him like

jade daggers. Her fist punched his left arm in a surprisingly strong blow. "Of course, I want this baby! Why do you thin—" She cut off her own words and drew her generous bottom lip up between her teeth.

Randy chose not to pursue what Scarlett didn't say; partly because his body cried out for warmth, partly because he didn't want to alienate her to the point that she'd take off again.

It wasn't up to him to interrogate her. Besides, something about the way she answered his pointed question—like a she–wolf defending her cub—redeemed her in his eyes. He felt a strong need to help her get that baby safely into the world.

"O–o–o–h!" Scarlett's tormented cry echoed through the snow-stilled night. She wrung a wad of his shirt in her hand so forcibly that Randy thanked God his chest hairs didn't get caught up in her fingers.

He watched in helpless silence as Scarlett dealt with the pain her baby inflicted. He reached out to steady her. She was not experiencing the first twinges of labor. She was having a teeth-gritting, complexion-bleaching, sweat-producing contraction!

He swallowed hard and glanced back at the disabled vehicle. He could call for help on the CB. The need to help Scarlett did *not* include witnessing the birth of her kid.

Hell, no!

Scarlett recovered and tried to push away from Randy. Something about her efforts to be so strong brought back the protective nature within him. Forgetting his qualms over her impending delivery, he drew her into the circle of his arms. She tried to fight him, but at last gave into the warmth and support he offered, leaning against him with a heavy sigh.

Hugging a pregnant woman was new to him. Getting his arms around her wasn't as hard as he expected. It felt as if they held a watermelon between them, but it wasn't a bad sensation. He stroked her hair back away from her face, realizing she'd left her cap and scarf in the truck. She'd have frozen to death before finding shelter, the little idiot.

"Are you okay?" he asked, gently.

"Do you care?" she hissed.

Randy growled and shook his head. She just couldn't be nice, could she? He'd had enough of this. They were wasting the warmth of the truck and the opportunity to contact an ambulance. Randy scooped her into his arms and headed for the truck.

"Good grief, woman!" he grunted. "What are you going to give birth to? An anchor?"

"I haven't gained that much weight," Scarlett defended herself, her voice a soft tremor against his neck.

Aw, now don't go crying on me! Randy's one big weakness was a woman's tears.

Scarlett swiped at a stray tear on her cheek before opening the door so he could deposit her on the passenger's seat.

Randy climbed into the truck, flipped up the generator switch, and smiled when the cab filled with light and a blast of warm air. "Now, isn't that much better?"

Scarlett huddled in the corner and sniffed.

Randy gripped the steering wheel with both hands and stared out the windshield. Her sniveling scraped over his spine the same as if it were fingernails down a blackboard. He had to stop her. "Ah . . . look, Scarlett. I don't know much about things like this. Hell, I don't know *anything* about this. It took me by surprise and . . . I'm . . . sorry for what I said. I mean that stuff about distracting me. You had nothing to do with that snowdrift."

Their eyes met briefly. His were hopeful he was on the right track. Hers were scornful and injured. He sighed and looked away.

"Anyway, I may have overreacted a bit—"

"Huh!" she scoffed.

He eyed her again. "And not been very sympathetic to your situation. It's just that—well, never mind. I'm just sorry, that's all." He rushed through the apology like a little boy hurrying through a confession of breaking a window with a baseball—as if he'd be absolved of his crime if it was admitted quickly. Jeez! He was no little boy. He turned to face Scarlett and found her shoulders bobbing up and down as she stared out the side window. His "grown-up" bravery shriveled.

Damn! She'd turned on all the faucets! Even Randy's most ardent apology didn't slow down the flow. He was way out of his league here. The women he kept company with never cried. They liked to have a good time and party and laugh. He'd never been serious with one of them and as a result, he possessed no experience in dealing with an emotional female.

He had to think of something—*anything*—to quell her tears.

"And," he continued, "I guess you aren't that big . . . I didn't know you were pregnant, did I?"

The sobs ceased.

Randy looked at Scarlett. Her head tilted toward him. Her smile rivaled Mona Lisa's. Diamond-bright tears clung to her lower lashes and her eyes glowed like sunlight through a sea mist.

Randy shook his head, amazed at where the woman's priorities lay. Apologizing for all his harsh words and accusations hadn't fazed her, but one subtle semi-compliment transformed her into an appealing sight.

Was there a man alive who understood a woman's mind?

Randy eyed Scarlett in trepidation as he listened to her breathe in short hisses. It seemed like the hundredth time in the last hour. She assured him the sound had nothing to do with him, but he wasn't convinced. Each time a contraction grabbed her, Scarlett focused upon him as her object of concentration while she breathed through the pain.

This whole birthing process resembled nothing Randy'd seen in the movies. It was a lot faster. A *whole* lot faster! Randy thought babies took their time, keeping their parents in suspense for as long as possible. Scarlett's baby was eager to enter the world. Boy, the kid was going to be surprised when he didn't enter a well-lit delivery room with all the modern conveniences and a roomful of people to applaud his arrival!

Randy thought there was plenty of time before the critical point. If a mottled, clammy complexion and perspiration drenched hair were any indication, they'd reached the critical point about half an hour ago. And those were *his* symptoms!

"Randy," Scarlett said, her husky voice now a soft rasp. "I–I don't understand. This isn't going at all like it's supposed to. This wasn't supposed to happen for hours after my water broke, and I was told labor could last for twelve or fifteen hours."

"*Fifteen* hours?! Jeez, I hope not." Shooting her a horrified look, he ran his hand along his suddenly stiff neck. "I can't last twelve or fifteen hours."

Scarlett blinked at him in flustered disbelief, then confessed, "I'm scared."

Randy studied her, wondering if his own eyes mirrored her worry. Too much was going wrong with this whole situation. The snow, the desolation, the stranded truck. He'd checked out that drift—a tree had fallen on the road and caused the snow to collect around it. That tree had snagged the front bumper and sent them into that wicked spin. Nothing seemed to work in their favor today.

Randy'd managed to start the engine, but any attempt to move the rig only buried it deeper into the ground. His attempts to call for help on the CB were useless. Of all nights for people to be sensible and get off the road, it had to be tonight. The CB could be broken for all he knew.

He didn't want to think about that.

Yet, he had to face facts. Scarlett's baby insisted on making an appearance as soon as possible. The longer it took to contact someone, the less time they had to be of any help. Randy knew *he* couldn't help Scarlett.

It wouldn't help matters to frighten her any more than she already was, however. He summoned up one of his most appealing smiles, draped one arm over the steering wheel, and rested his other hand on the top of her head, massaging her moist hair with his thumb.

"Now, don't worry. We'll be rescued long before the baby comes."

"I don't think so!" Scarlett managed as she shot upward in the seat, an agonizing wave of pain waging war on her lower body. Her face reddened with strain and powerful discomfort. Her eyes squeezed shut and her jaw clamped together as she swallowed a scream.

Randy yanked the CB to his mouth and yelled, "Mayday! Mayday! I need help, do you hear me?! Is there a medical person out there?! Mayday!"

The CB sputtered in nerve-snapping silence. No one could hear him. Not even one of "North Carolina's Finest." Randy recalled the many times Ol' Smokey had stopped him in the past just for routine harassment, and now there wasn't one within hearing distance.

Randy's body sagged.

"Mayday?" Dixie's voice filled the cab.

Randy's head and spirits lifted. "Dixie?"

"Mayday? What's a good ol' boy doing using mayday?"

"This good ol' boy needs a doctor."

Dixie's attitude shifted. "Are you hurt? Did you run off the road? Why didn't you just pull over to a restaurant, like I did?"

Randy expelled a long breath. He'd have to answer her questions before they could get to the meat of this sandwich. "I'm not hurt. I did run off the road and the closest thing to a restaurant around here is a squirrel's hoard of nuts."

"Well, if you ain't hurt, then why do you need a doctor?"

"That hitchhiker—the teenage boy I was going to return to his parents—is named Scarlett and she's in the middle of childbirth."

Dixie left them in silence for a long time. Then her laughter chimed through the radio. "The confirmed bachelor, the Romeo of the open road, the Casanova of the CB is going to deliver a baby?"

"I'm not going to deliver this baby, Dixie."

"*Sure* you aren't."

"I'm not."

Dixie sighed. "Has her water broken?"

Randy eyed Scarlett as she came out of another contraction. "Unfortunately, yes."

"Hm–m–m. How far apart are her contractions?"

"They aren't." Randy knew he'd gain nothing by lying.

"Is your truck disabled?"

"Buried up to the axles."

"Then roll up your sleeves, boy, and call yourself a midwife!"

Randy interrupted her laughter. "Dixie, that's not funny!"

"Wasn't meant to be. I'm just stating the facts."

"Well, I'll state a fact. I don't know nothing about birthing ba—"

Before Randy could complete the line from the famous movie, Scarlett's fingers gripped his arm. "Spare me, will you?!"

Randy smiled weakly and shrugged, then spoke into the CB, "Help me, Dixie."

"Give me a few minutes and I'll see if I can't get an ambulance out there for you."

"Thank you."

Randy wanted to breath easier, but he knew he wouldn't until Scarlett was in an ambulance on the way to Cape Fear Hospital, preferably with the baby still in her belly.

But, at least he'd established contact with Dixie and he didn't feel quite as helpless.

He looked at Scarlett. She was hissing again. Her long hair was beginning to resemble a well-used mop. The mottled crimson hue of her skin buried her burnt sienna freckles and made her wide, green eyes seem like spots of vegetation in a forest fire.

Randy couldn't remember the last time Scarlett's color had been normal and her face pain free.

"Dixie will get us some help, Scarlett. Everything will be all right. Don't worry." He wasn't sure if he was reassuring Scarlett or himself.

Scarlett nodded and sucked in long, deep breaths before another contraction hit her.

Randy never knew a few minutes could be so long. He felt as if Scarlett's kid should be in college by the time Dixie returned.

"Star."

"Dixie! What did you find out? When's help arriving?"

"Well, I have some good news and some bad news."

Randy groaned. Scarlett's expression became fearful.

"I think I'll tell you the bad news first, then the good news will seem better. The ambulance isn't coming."

"The ambulance isn't coming?" Randy and Scarlett shouted together.

"Not for awhile, anyway. There's a huge pile-up on 117. Lots of cars and lots of seriously injured people. All medical help is occupied with getting them to the hospital. They say they'll send an ambulance out as soon as they can spare one."

"As soon as they can *spare* one?! We have a pregnant woman here who's about to give birth—let me emphasize about—and they can't spare an ambulance?"

"Star, those people are *seriously* injured. Trauma patients. They aren't going to pull any ambulances away from them because of one little baby being born. Sorry to put it that way, but babies were born for thousands of years before there ever was a doctor or an ambulance."

"But they weren't born in the cab of my truck." Randy and Scarlett looked at each other, both silently expressing their concern.

"You're right, but you have to realize the importance of their decision. Besides, they wouldn't move Scarlett if her water's broken and her contractions are so close, anyway. That baby's going to be born in your truck no matter what." Amusement re-entered Dixie's voice.

"But there'd be someone here besides me to deliver it," Randy pointed out.

"Which brings us to the good news—I was a nurse for eight years and I have three kids of my own. I'll talk you through the delivery."

"*That's* the good news, Dix? I was hoping for an alternate plan. Like a helicopter or snowmobile, maybe."

Scarlett groaned and Randy lowered his head to the steering wheel.

"Why did I get up this morning?" he asked out loud.

"How far is she dilated?" Dixie questioned him.

Randy's head jerked up. "How the hell would I know?"

"You haven't looked?"

Randy shifted in his seat, flustered and embarrassed. "I wouldn't know what I was looking at."

"That's not what I hear," Dixie returned.

Randy evaded Scarlett's eyes, suddenly hating his Don Juan image he'd let get out of hand. He didn't realize just how far out until today. In the past, his reputation had served him well. But now, Dixie was talking babies and birth and doing things to a near stranger that had nothing to do with passion. He found the whole thing humiliating for himself as well as Scarlett, but Dixie found his discomfort amusing!

Dixie was his lifeline, however. Randy wasn't going to risk ruffling her feathers just because he felt a little squeamish about delivering a baby and a little perturbed over Dixie's not taking his uneasiness seriously.

"Do you have some liquor?" Dixie asked.

"If I did, I'd be drunk by now," Randy returned.

"I have some," Scarlett told him.

He eyed her.

"It was a present. You never know when it might come in handy," she explained and pointed to one of her bags. "It's in that one."

Randy gave Scarlett another appraising scan before he rummaged through her odd assortment of belongings. His fingers closed around a cool bottle of Jack Daniels. "I have a pint of Jack Daniels, Dixie."

"Good. Pour some over your hands."

"But it's Black Label!" Randy protested.

"Just do it! And be sure to rub it all over your hands and way past your wrists."

As he mumbled about wasting good whiskey, Randy poured some of the liquor over his hands and wrists. He thought about taking a long gulp of the liquid then decided against it. They might need more later.

"All right. It's done," he grumbled. "Now what?"

"Good," Dixie praised him. "She has to be dilated ten centimeters for the baby to come. That's about four fingers."

"Uh–uh. I don't like the sound of this!" Randy could feel his color beginning to match Scarlett's.

"Uh–*huh*!" Dixie's tone was becoming charged with humor again and her obvious delight added to his sense of doom. If Dixie found it funny, it meant something embarrassing to him.

Randy didn't dare look at Scarlett. He'd seen women naked and never batted an eye. In fact, he'd hardly blinked sometimes for fear he'd miss something. He'd touched every inch of feminine flesh known to man and been bold about it at times. But what he predicted Dixie was going to tell him to do to Scarlett left him as tongue-tied and red-faced as a youthful virgin.

Dixie continued, "Now, Star, to find out how far she's dilated, you must first do something I hear you do very well—remove her underwear . . ."

THREE

"Scarlett," Randy said, raising his eyes over the mound of her stomach. "This has got to hurt."

"That's an understatement," she replied through clenched teeth, as another contraction finally began to subside. She met his eyes for just a moment, catching his concerned expression. She licked her parched lips and said, "Want to trade places?"

Randy had no desire to. He'd scrounged around for items to transform the truck into a makeshift delivery room, then transferred Scarlett to the driver's side so he'd have more space to work. He'd watched her strain and huff and puff. Watching was enough for him. That examination of Scarlett was *more* than any trucking cowboy should have to endure!

The initial "crowning" of the baby's head had produced an exciting patch of dark hair, but even that thrill fizzled because nothing else had happened for awhile now. With nothing else to do, Randy thought.

Things sure would be a lot different right now if he could have afforded a truck with a fully-equipped sleeper and a microwave and shower. One with a king-sized bed capable of accommodating a rotund mother-to-be. *Those* sleepers had doorways leading to them. *His* truck only had a slit between the seats. A mighty small slit at that. When he'd tried to slip Scarlett into the sleeping space, she'd belted him. *That* was when he'd made the driver's seat into a birthing chair.

Randy tried to understand the philosophy behind childbirth and couldn't quite figure it out. He knew the technical aspect of the process, even liked a few choice segments of it. He just couldn't grasp what possessed a woman to put herself through this! Willingly! And often more than once!

The maternal instinct was a strong drive—stronger than the need for food or water—if women happily accepted having something the size of a small beer keg shoved down a passageway the size of a beer bottleneck.

Or was it deep love for the father of the baby?

Randy eyed Scarlett and wondered if she loved her baby's father. He also wondered where the hell the bastard was! If Randy had someone going through this for him, he'd be there, by God!

I am here.

But none of this had anything to do with him except that he was the poor sucker delivering another man's baby.

"Randy!" Scarlett cried out, her voice hoarse with urgency.

"What?" Randy snapped out of his thoughts and looked into her wide, scared eyes. She was panting so hard she should have hyperventilated long ago. "What's wrong, Scarlett?"

"S—Something very different is happening!" She leaned forward, panting heavily.

Randy looked down and exclaimed, "You're damned right! Have mercy!"

He didn't need Dixie's experienced opinion to tell him the baby was coming—right *now*! The head began to emerge at an accelerated rate.

"Dixie! It's happening!" Randy said into the CB, then shoved it at Scarlett. "Here, hold this."

Scarlett backhanded the CB, sending it crashing to the floor.

"Why'd you do that?! You could break it!" Randy shouted.

"I don't give a damn about that CB!" Scarlett snarled.

"It's the only link we have to Dixie!"

"Who the hell cares?! She's not here!" Scarlett lurched forth to push, crying out in agony.

Her simple words of wisdom and pain-filled shriek brought Randy back to his senses. They *were* all alone in this. Maybe Dixie was on the CB, but she couldn't really help if they ran into a problem. It was up to Scarlett and the baby and—Lord have mercy—him!

He tried to remember everything Dixie told him. Utmost was slowing down the baby's exit from Scarlett's body since he couldn't perform an episiotomy, whatever the hell that was. The technique left something to be desired as Dixie explained it, but now he plunged in and aimed all his concentration on the task.

Scarlett seized the steering wheel with one hand and the edge of her seat with the other, straining until the contraction peaked. Lying back against the pillows Randy'd shoved behind her, she swallowed and declared, "This is *the* most embarrassing thing that's ever happened to me!"

Randy allowed himself one glance up from his ministrations. "With everything else there is to worry about, you're suddenly modest?"

His scoffing rankled her and she retorted, "It's not every day I have a stranger shove his hands—"

"I know what I'm doing, dammit!" He interrupted, feeling his face burn as red as hers. "Jeez, Scarlett! We have to do this, but we don't have to talk about it!"

"Ah! Damn!" Scarlett rose with another contraction and Randy was almost thankful because it ended their discussion.

Everything began to move too fast for them to carry on a conversation, anyway. He looked down, mesmerized by the event unfolding before his eyes.

"The head's almost out!" Randy announced after Scarlett made another surging push. He looked up with a smile, then frowned at Scarlett's hands gripping the seat and steering wheel. She strained like a weightlifter performing a five-hundred-pound jerk. She seemed perfectly capable of twisting those truck parts into a useless mass of metal and upholstery.

Randy watched Scarlett for a moment then concentrated on the baby. The baby. That was the important thing right now.

Scarlett screamed as the baby's head eased from her body and a shoulder appeared. Randy gritted his teeth against the sound of her torture. He wished there was something he could do to help her. He'd never seen anyone go through this much pain before.

Scarlett was working hard now. Pumping, pushing, panting, crying out in pain. She leaned back during each miniscule reprieve, exhausted and perspiring, only to begin the whole process over with no adequate recuperation period.

Her fortitude was waning fast. Randy wondered how she'd managed to last this long and where she'd find the strength to complete the delivery.

He wiped sweat from his eyes with the back of his wrist. "One more shoulder to go, Scarlett. Push real hard."

"I'm pushing as hard as I can, damn you!" But she pushed anyway and the other shoulder appeared. She fell back again, heaving in precious air and closing her eyes in pain.

"One more push, Scarlett."

Scarlett's eyes opened. "I hate men!"

Randy ignored her remark. He was surprised it hadn't been more caustic. She was really getting tired if that was the best she could do. He egged her on. "Come on, Scarlett! Push! Dammit! I sure as hell can't do this for you!"

"I hate you!" Scarlett's face was the epitome of determination and anger as she pulled herself up again. Sucking in a huge breath, she held it and used every morsel of her remaining strength to bear down one last time.

Scarlett trembled and struggled to expel the infant. Randy gave her a lot of credit. She wasn't going to let up until it was over and the pain stopped.

Randy, vaguely aware of lights flashing and unfamiliar noises, couldn't look away. Nothing could be more worthy of his attention than what he witnessed right now. He offered gentle encouragement, "Come on, Scarlett. It's almost over."

As soon as the words left Randy's lips, the baby slid into his waiting hands. Randy gulped in stunned silence.

Scarlett collapsed in exhausted glory, tears of joy and relief streaking her freckled, splotched face. She laughed and cried at the same time when the baby's protesting screams filled the cab.

As Randy gave the baby a quick cleaning and wrapped it in a blanket from his sleeper, he listed the details for Scarlett. "Two arms and legs . . . ten fingers . . . ten toes . . . great set of lungs . . . no teeth, though."

"Would you tell us what it is?" Dixie's voice came up from the floor where the CB rested.

Randy moved over Scarlett, beaming with a pride he didn't understand, and lay her baby in her arms. Keeping his eyes on Scarlett, he grabbed the radio and announced, "By the way, it's a girl."

Dixie and what sounded like an entire convoy of truckers let out a loud whoop.

Scarlett's gaze darted to Randy, wiping away the smile he'd been wearing. There was a look in her eyes, a look that made him feel as if he sat beside a cozy fireplace instead of crouched in a cramped truck cab in the middle of a snowstorm. Scarlett's loveliness at that moment took his breath away.

Randy couldn't quite put his finger on what made her enchanting. Her face was blotchy except for where it was pale. A film of pure, unladylike sweat covered her skin and held her hair captive against her face and neck.

But she radiated a euphoric glow which illuminated the truck and his insides.

"A girl?" Scarlett smiled down at her daughter then looked at Randy. "Thank you. Thank you so much!"

Randy swallowed. Such earnest appreciation in her husky voice left him feeling inadequate. He didn't know how to deal with the look in her eyes and the gratitude in her voice. Especially since he was an unwilling hero in the first place.

His gaze fell to the baby. She looked as worn out as her mother, but her huckleberry-blue eyes caught his attention. She regarded her new world with a smug curiosity and the astuteness of an old sage.

Randy'd never seen a newborn baby—not one this fresh, anyway—and he wondered if maybe everyone was born with the wisdom of the ages, losing a little of it with each passing year. This infant sure looked as if she had a few aces in the hole when it came to intelligence.

The door behind Randy opened, a gust of frigid air forcing him to swing around and glare at the intruders. Relief and a strange measure of regret flooded over him when he discovered a state trooper and two paramedics peering inside the cab.

One paramedic asked, "You folks need some help?"

Randy looked back at Scarlett. No longer sheathed in privacy, her skin burned crimson and her eyes looked in every direction except at him. He pulled the blanket down over Scarlett's exposed legs, feeling a bit embarrassed by the strangers himself.

Strangers. Weren't he and Scarlett strangers? Not anymore, and he wasn't referring to the fact that he knew just a little too much about her anatomy now. *That* part made them uncomfortable. What they'd just shared wiped away the formalities. They were now co-workers, partners, accomplices in a deed Randy couldn't help but admit was pretty spectacular.

The intimacy of the moment broken, Randy moved away from Scarlett and nodded. "We could have really used it about two hours ago."

"The tow truck should be here any time," the trooper, a man in his late forties, announced. He'd reluctantly radioed for a wrecker when Randy informed him he'd sleep in his truck before he'd leave it. Officer Martin, muttering something about "blackmailing him with writing up a death report," radioed for a wrecker and forced Randy to sit inside the patrol car while the paramedics took care of Scarlett.

Randy nodded, his eyes remaining on his rig. "Thanks."

"Your truck's really stuck and it's hard to tell how much damage there is. I don't know how you missed plowing right over that tree. You're very lucky," the trooper commented. "I don't know when I've ever seen a rig run off the road and not roll over, even if it didn't have a trailer attached."

Randy didn't either. Over the years, he'd heard of too many people meeting their end that way. Rigs could be real unsteady at times—no matter what the conditions or how good the driver.

"I'd say it was something like a miracle," the trooper added.

"Yeah, there were a lot of miracles going on today," Randy said. *What's taking so long with Scarlett?*

As if answering his silent question, the paramedics lowered Scarlett and her baby onto a stretcher and carried them toward the ambulance.

Randy jumped out of the patrol car and joined them at the back door of the rescue vehicle.

"Randy," Scarlett said, reaching for his hand.

His fingers automatically curled about her slender, warm hand and, he thought, it felt so good to touch her. "How . . . are you?"

She smiled. "We're both doing fine."

"You did a great job," one of the paramedics told him. "They're both in good shape." He glanced at the rig. "Wish I could say the same thing about your truck . . . Maybe some bleach would clean it up?"

Randy felt queasy again. He might as well burn the truck and start all over. When he looked down at Scarlett, she looked just as nauseous.

"I'm so sorry," she said, her bottom lip quivering and her eyes beginning to moisten.

"It's okay." *Don't cry!* "I have insurance. Besides, maybe the damage won't be so bad."

No one concurred with that optimistic statement and Scarlett told him, "I just wish there was some way to pay you for all your trouble."

"I don't know anyone that rich," he joked.

She smiled instead of returning the acid comeback he expected. Her face clouded. "I suppose this is good-bye, then."

Randy lifted a corner of the blanket Scarlett held and gazed down at the wrinkled, squirming bundle beneath it. "What's her name?"

"Hannah Grace."

His brows raised and his eyes rounded. "Hannah?"

"Yes, it means given to much grace, mercy and prayer." Her pleased smile faded when she noticed his sour expression. "What's wrong with it?"

He sensed her defensiveness building and shook his head. "Nothing! Nothing at all." *If you're eighty years old.* "Mind if I call her Hank?"

Scarlett smiled.

"Folks," the paramedic at Scarlett's feet broke in, "I hate to interrupt, but we should be going."

Scarlett fell into a solemn mood. "Good-bye, Randy. I'll never forget you."

He knew he could be old and senile and he'd remember this night. "Good-bye, Scarlett."

Once Scarlett and Hank were safely inside the ambulance, one of the men urged Randy, "That checkup I gave you wasn't that extensive for the kind of jolt you went through. At least drop by to see your doctor and have him do a thorough checkup."

Randy nodded just so the man would leave him alone.

As the taillights of the ambulance became red pin dots on the horizon, Randy found being free of Scarlett didn't give him the rush he anticipated. She was irrational at times and even a tad dangerous, but she had her moments when she could be mighty appealing. And even when she was unappealing, she wasn't dull. It'd been a long time since he'd met a female who was capable of running his emotions through such a gauntlet.

"Hey!" Trooper Martin shouted from his car. "You are bound and determined to make me fill out a death report tonight, aren't you? Get in the car before you freeze!"

After one more glance up the road, Randy stuffed his hand into the pockets of his faded jeans and ambled to the car.

Two days later, Randy approached the nurses' station on the main floor of Cape Fear Hospital and prayed he saw no one he knew. Randy Taylor on the OB/GYN floor was enough to foster a year's worth of rumors in Dominion. Cape Fear was in Wilmington and Wilmington was a lot bigger than Dominion, so the odds were in his favor of not being recognized. He didn't mind being blamed for the existence of every baby in the nursery—being seen with this overgrown bouquet bothered him.

Relieving that street vendor of an entire bucket of multicolored blossoms seemed like a good idea when he did it.

Now, as he shifted the arrangement to one hand and met the curious brown eyes of a young nurse, he felt downright foolish.

"May I help you?" she asked, her mouth twitching with an unreleased smile.

"Uh . . . I was looking for Scarlett Kincaid's room."

Her gaze swept over him with interest. "Are you a relative?"

She was fishing. She couldn't possibly think he was Hank's father. Surely the man had shown up by now!

"No," he responded flatly.

"A friend? A *good* friend?"

The woman was as smooth as sandpaper.

Randy leaned an elbow on the counter and gave her his most heated stare. "Ms. Kincaid and I have shared the most intimate, exhilarating, exhausting experience a man and woman can share."

His silky-nightgowns-and-soft-lights voice floated over her and she licked her lips.

Randy straightened. "I delivered her baby."

"Oh, *you're* Randy Taylor." Then she answered his silent question. "Scarlett told us all about you."

Randy groaned. "Don't believe a word that madwoman says."

The nurse grinned. "Oh? Listening to her, you should have floated in here . . . after you parted a sea or something equally miraculous."

Randy could feel just how stupid his smile looked. He knew he thrust out his chest a bit too far, but he couldn't help it. Scarlett thought he was a saint.

The nurse came around the counter and tilted her head up at him. "Don't preen too much, cowboy. Women tend to feel gratitude to the person who helps them through childbirth." She pointed to a man in his early sixties who would reach midway up Randy's chest. His gray hair looked as if someone tossed a firecracker in it and his clothes as if they hadn't seen the underside of an iron since the day they were manufactured two decades ago. "That's Dr. Baxter and half the patients on this floor are in love with him. You're in great company, huh?" She winked.

Randy's cheeks burned. Okay, so he wasn't so great after all.

"Scarlett's room is that way. First door on the left. She hasn't had any visitors . . . I'm sure she'll like the flowers."

As Randy walked down the hall, he tried to remember why he came. He considered leaving the bouquet with that nurse and running for the safety of Preston's Bar and Grill in Dominion.

He wouldn't do that, of course. Especially since that nurse told him Scarlett'd had no visitors.

Randy just didn't know anything about visiting a woman in the hospital, not one he'd seen the way he'd seen Scarlett.

He had to *talk* to Scarlett while he was in her room. And so far, the only thing they had in common was his wrecked truck and her delivering a child in that wrecked truck. Neither fact lent itself to easy conversation.

Shallow as it sounded, he seldom talked to a woman when there wasn't a sexual reason behind it.

It was just that these last two days had been . . . well . . . *weird*. Thinking back on the birth only brought good memories, proud memories. He'd not passed out during Hank's entrance. He'd done pretty damn good considering the circumstances. Though he didn't want to do it again, he was kind of glad he'd experienced a birth once in his life.

What disturbed him were those dreams! They centered around a freckled blonde bearing a strong resemblance to Scarlett. They alternated between upliftingly holy and sinfully erotic. He'd taken more cold showers in the last two days than he'd taken in his entire life.

He didn't need one woman taking up so much of his time—physically or mentally.

Absence made the heart grow fonder, Randy'd always heard.

His separation, however, erased *all* of Scarlett's offensive qualities. Maybe this visit would overdose him on her acid tongue and irritating personality, and he'd leave the hospital properly purged of Scarlett Kincaid.

Entering the room the nurse pointed out as Scarlett's, Randy felt as if something slammed into his chest. The woman lying in the bed near the window couldn't be Scarlett!

Washed in the pale, late-December sunlight, she looked like a smudged pastel drawing. Her hair spread across the pillow, a fan of silky palomino strands. Her skin, what he could see of it, was transparent with rosy undertones, instead of the mass of blotches and splotches he remembered.

Her head was turned toward the window in what appeared to be deep concentration or heavy slumber.

When she swatted at a tear, he knew she wasn't sleeping.

What could possibly be wrong?

Hank.

Something had to be wrong with Hank! That was the only thing he could figure would have turned on Scarlett's faucet; unless someone had commented about her weight again, of course.

Randy recalled the women he'd seen around the nursery window when he walked by it. He'd noticed a few women shuffling down the hall cooing at the pink or blue bundles in their arms. Scarlett wasn't holding a bundle nor watching one through the window.

Dammit! Something was wrong with Hank and that blasted nurse hadn't even mentioned it!

Randy bolted from the doorway and stomped toward the bed. "Hey!"

Scarlett's attentions shifted to the owner of the masculine bellow and the boot heels striking the tile floor.

Randy!

He tromped toward her like a bull after a red bandanna and, despite her apprehensions and fears, it was good to see him. It wasn't smart for him to *be* there, but it was good to see him.

Of course, it hadn't been smart for Scarlett to crawl into his truck in the first place. Over the last two days, she'd replayed the entire scene with Randy and became ill at how easily her wall of caution had crumbled.

She'd been so careful for seven and a half months, not only with her life, but with others as well. In less than ten minutes she'd not only jumped into the truck, but told Randy her real name. Her *real* name, for pete's sake! How many pregnant Scarlett Kincaids could there be, anyway? With that one morsel of truth, she could have signed her death warrant . . . or Randy's.

At first, she thought it might be her life on the line. After all, Randy's appearance on that deserted stretch of highway was just a little too coincidental. If she hadn't been in labor, alarms might have sounded in her head and she'd have disappeared into the snowstorm. Of course, she and Hannah would have frozen to death.

Even if Randy had been a part of the nightmare Scarlett had lived for so long, she had to thank him for Hannah anyway. But a few hours ago it dawned on her that he had sure given an Oscar-winning performance in the truck if he was a threat to her. She had nothing to fear from Randy, and that meant he had everything to fear from her.

Although the look in his eyes was menacing, it probably had nothing to do with why she'd been on the run and everything to do with his truck.

He was going to kill her . . . and he'd brought a *lot* of flowers to toss over her mangled body.

There wasn't a whole lot she could do to save herself. Randy blocked the only exit out of the room except for the window. Crawling out the first-floor window wouldn't kill her, but, in her condition, she'd never muster up a decent trot. She might as well lie back and relax. There was something refreshing about the thought of cheating Jonas Kincaid out of killing her.

Scarlett eyed Randy. He seemed different from what she remembered. The arms that so easily lifted her and carried her back to the truck weren't those of a weight lifter at all. They were normal arms. Normal length. Normal circumference.

The hands that brought Hannah into the world weren't comparable to a world famous surgeon nor a faith healer. They were nice hands. Long, slender fingers. Manly, squared palms. All pleasing, but not gold-plated.

His shoulders hadn't brushed the jambs when he stormed through the door. Randy Taylor was just a man, plain and simple.   Or . . . was he? His face, ruggedly angular, was precisely chiseled. His cheeks and jawbones were well-defined, but softened by smooth skin which retained a slight tan from summer. The straight line of his nose drew her attention to the dark brown brows drawn together in angry concentration.

No matter how irate the rest of his face appeared, his mouth ruined the picture. His lips begged to be kissed. They lured a woman's finger to them. Their well-sculpted suppleness could quicken any female heartbeat.

His eyes were most compelling. They were a blinding blue, brilliant in contrast to his dark hair and curly, brown lashes. The outside corners drooped just enough to make them sexy . . . bedroom eyes.

Randy's thighs collided with the side of the bed and he began his interrogation. "What's wrong? Where's Hank? Why are you crying?"

Scarlett ran her hands across her forgotten tears and answered, "Hannah's in the nursery."

Randy flushed. "Nursery?"

Scarlett nodded. "I just fed her and now she's sleeping."

"Sleeping?"

"Yes, sleeping. Babies do a lot of that."

"Sleeping." Randy cleared his throat and turned away from her as he considered what she said. "Well . . . ah . . . I saw everyone else with their babies or standing at the nursery . . . and . . ." He began to pace the floor to release some nervous energy. He waved his arms as he spoke, expelling a few blue and pink petals from the huge bouquet. He scooped them from the floor, stopping in mid-bend to look at Scarlett. She was smiling that damned Mona Lisa smile again! He must have done *something* good, although he couldn't for the life of him decide what that was. He only knew that when she smiled like that he felt the same as if he'd appeared at Preston's Bar minus his jeans.

Feeling stupid for drawing incorrect conclusions about Hank, he snapped, "Why the hell were you crying if Hank's okay?"

She couldn't tell him she cried because she feared for his life. She couldn't tell him she cried because she feared for her own life. So she used the age-old excuse. "New mothers always cry."

"Oh . . ." Randy stood up straight and eyed her. "I see." He didn't really, he just didn't want to pursue the mental mechanics of this woman. Not much had changed inside her head since they'd last seen each other. He'd be an old man before he figured out where her hood latch was located. He shoved the flowers at her. "Here."

Scarlett took the flowers with both hands as Randy removed his fleece-lined denim jacket and draped it over the bedside chair. When he looked back at her, he knew this visit had been a mistake.

Witnessing Scarlett's face brighten—glow might be a better description—as she smelled the bouquet did nothing to renew his faded memories of her cantankerous spirit. She wasn't being irritating at all. She was being . . . charming.

Her green gaze fell upon him. "Thank you."

Randy surveyed the room. It was a nice enough space, he decided. The muted wall colors were contrasted by a bright pinkish, purplish, bluish bedspread. Women knew the proper names of those colors because they appreciated them. A bright red would have suited him better.

What Randy noticed most were the things missing from the room. Flowers. Cards. A proud papa holding Scarlett's hand.

"I . . . didn't expect you to come see me," Scarlett said looking over the flowers at him.

Randy glanced down at her, then lowered himself onto the chair because he needed something to do. "Well, I wanted to see how Hank was. After all, I did have a little to do with her being here."

"Oh." Scarlett said in a small voice and examined the bouquet.

He could see her disappointment. "And I wanted to know you were all right."

She flashed him a grateful smile. "I'm fine. How's your truck?"

"One of us had a guardian angel. There was no major damage. It's muddy as hell and it needs some minor adjustments, but for what it's been through, it's in good shape." He shook his head in amazement. "That says something for Peterbilt, I guess."

"And . . . the inside?" she ventured, her voice a husky whisper. Her face flamed red with embarrassment from just how much he knew about her.

"Well, the inside's another story, but we're working on it."

Their eyes met for a brief moment, but that was all she could take and averted her eyes. "I swear I didn't know I was in labor. I'd been walking most of the day. The snow made it harder to walk and I guess I was just so cold and tired . . . I really didn't recognize what was happening. They tell me I'm, well, more or less, made for this sort of thing. My baby would have come fairly fast for a first anyway. That, combined with the extra physical exertion, just worked against us.''

Scarlett looked at Randy and he nodded. Then she flushed and slightly shook her head as if trying to shoo away painful memories. ''If you'll give me your address, I promise I'll send you money for the damages as soon as I can.''

Randy blinked at her. This wasn't helping him one bit! Where was the chubby street urchin with the abrasive conversational techniques and borderline dementia he expected to find?

A vulnerable, lovely creature possessed Scarlett Kincaid's body. Oh, no, this would do nothing to get him back to sleep-filled nights and warm showers.

He cleared his throat. ''You don't have to pay me back, Scarlett. You couldn't help going into labor and the rest was an accident.''

Scarlett knocked another tear from her cheek and changed the subject. ''Have you seen Hannah?''

Randy shook his head. Standing at the nursery window speaking in undignified gibberish just wasn't his style.

''She's beautiful,'' Scarlett told him.

''I'm sure she is.''

The room fell silent. Randy felt awkward. He'd already studied the interior decorating as much as any self-respecting man could handle. He had found out for himself that Scarlett and her baby were the epitome of health. He'd also discovered that much more time alone with this woman and he could permanently disconnect the hot water line to his shower. It was time for him to go.

''Well, gotta go.'' He pushed himself off the chair and smoothed down his worn jeans.

''So soon?'' Scarlett looked up at him, disappointed.

''Yup. Dixie's waiting at some truck stop for me to tell her how you're doing.'' It was a lie, pure and simple. Dixie wasn't waiting anywhere for him. He had no idea where she was right now. He'd just used her as an excuse to get away from Scarlett. Not in the habit of telling untruths, this one didn't taste very good on Randy's tongue.

"Oh . . . Tell her I said thank you for everything. She was very nice to help us."

"She knows I'd have hunted her down if she didn't."

That made Scarlett smile. "Randy, why did she call you Star?"

Randy pulled on his jacket. "My CB handle's Lone Star."

"Because you come from Texas?"

"Because I'm a loner."

Scarlett's smile drooped into a frown for a moment before her expression brightened again. "Thank you for coming and for the flowers."

She touched one of the delicate blossoms and Randy took a giant step toward the door. He wasn't going to think about how she and the flower possessed the same fragility. No sirree!

"You take it easy, Scarlett."

He left the room quickly, but stopped two steps down the hall when he spotted the nursery window. A white-haired couple walked away, leaving it vacant.

He deserved one look, didn't he? Glancing around, he saw no one who might have the same destination in mind and headed for the window.

Seven babies, including a set of twins, snuggled in their hospital-issued blankets. Before he could locate Hank, two nurses joined him.

"See, there she is. On the third row," one nurse said, pointing. "That's the Kincaid baby."

Randy followed the nurse's direction and stepped closer to the window as he stared at Hank. She slept in a fetal position, her little fists balled tightly and her mouth moving in a sucking motion. An abundance of dark, auburn hair covered her tiny head and she possessed the cutest pug nose he'd ever seen.

"Isn't she the most adorable baby?" the first nurse asked.

Randy and the other nurse agreed. Her response was verbal. His was a nod.

"Too bad about her circumstances, though."

Randy fought the urge to swing around and interrogate the woman. He spread a hand against the glass and gazed at Hank as he suspected all sorts of genetic problems.

"What circumstances?" the second nurse asked.

"Well, her poor mother has no money, no job, and no one to turn to."

"That's a lot to face with a newborn!"

"I know," the first nurse agreed. "I don't think I'd be holding up as well as that poor woman. She has nowhere to go except the streets when she leaves here."

Randy's jaw tightened. The hand flattened against the glass involuntarily bunched into a fist. His ears rang so much he couldn't tell if the nurses continued their conversation or fell silent. He thought he heard that the refuge centers were full and something about welfare, but everything became fuzzy.

Damn Scarlett! Why hadn't she confided in him?

And damn him because he just *had* to get a peek at the infant!

Randy whirled about and aimed himself at the nearest outside door. He needed air.

The women shook hands as they watched Randy leave. The brown-eyed nurse who'd directed Randy to Scarlett's room joined them.

"Well?" she asked. "Think he'll be back?"

"With a car seat and a teddy bear," one of the others told her.

The three of them smiled like cats who'd found an endless supply of cream, satisfied that their plan appeared to have worked.

FOUR

Randy wondered why he hadn't left the giant pink teddy bear in his pickup along with the infant carseat.

He felt ridiculous.

He looked ridiculous! Every eye in the crowded hospital lobby was upon him, he just knew it. That whispering couple in the corner was snickering at him for sure.

Well, he couldn't blame them.

He checked his watch and sighed. The brown-eyed nurse he met yesterday told him Scarlett and Hank would be released at eleven. Now, at a quarter to twelve, he'd seen no sign of them. How long did it take to pack two shoulder bags, sign some papers, and wrap up a six-pound newborn, anyway?

Nothing should have gone wrong at the discharge desk. He'd spent the better part of yesterday afternoon seeing to that. Without an appointment, he'd waited an hour and a half to talk to one of the hospital's collections counselors, and it took another twenty-five minutes to start the ball rolling on a payment plan Scarlett might be able to afford.

Babies were damned expensive little creatures! If Scarlett had delivered Hank in the hospital instead of the truck, they'd have to put the kid on layaway!

57

A noisy entourage entered the lobby, capturing everyone's attention. Randy gave a sigh of relief to see Scarlett among the group.

His stomach immediately knotted at the confrontation he knew would occur once Scarlett heard his proposition . . .

Bad choice of words. Offer? Yeah, offer.

A blonde nurse's aide carried the brown vinyl bags holding Scarlett's belongings. A brunette was in charge of the still-perky bouquet Randy'd presented Scarlett the day before. The nurse carrying Hank cooed to the child in the language only those who loved children could speak or translate.

An orderly pushed Scarlett's wheelchair. A strapping young man with biceps the size of steamship rounds, he seemed more suited to splitting logs than escorting new moms to the door. Seeing the expression of pure pleasure on his face from being surrounded by so many females, Randy understood why the man held onto this job.

Scarlett remained detached from the chaos that occurred when babies and ladies came together. She clutched the handle of a pink bag resting on her lap and watched blocks of the tile floor pass beneath her chair.

When they stopped inside the lobby, Scarlett's head lifted and her green gaze fell upon Randy.

He felt like a fool standing there with the oversized stuffed bear under his arm and shifted his weight self-consciously from one foot to the other.

"Randy?" Scarlett managed to say through her surprise. Every time she thought they'd said good-bye, he showed up again. She was happy to see him each time, but had started to wonder what these reappearances were leading to. When would the bomb drop? "Wha–What are you doing here?"

He stepped forward and grinned. "Hey!"

She eyed the bear then compared its size to her daughter's.

Okay, the bear's too big and I feel like an idiot. "She can grow into it," Randy said with a shrug.

Scarlett stared at him, expecting an answer to her question.

No sense beating around the bush. "I've come to take you home."

Her forehead creased in confusion. "But I have no—. Wait a minute. *Whose* home?"

"Mine, of course."

"Yours?" Scarlett bolted from the chair with such force everyone surrounding her scattered. When she doubled over in agony with the next breath, they gathered about her again, concern on all their faces.

Scarlett glanced about the densely populated lobby. With such an audience, she couldn't grip the actual part of her anatomy which caused all the pain. So, with a few under-the-breath curses, she settled for hugging her abdomen.

The orderly aimed the chair beneath Scarlett and with everyone's help—too much help, really—she collapsed onto it. "Bad move!" she declared. "That was a bad move!"

Scarlett glared at Randy. He'd just dropped the bomb and she felt an overwhelming disappointment. How silly of her for thinking he might be different! He wanted to help her all right, but he wanted some action in return. Was he perverted or just chauvinistic? She hoped for the latter and attacked it.

"So, Mr. Macho! You expected me to leap at the chance to live with you!"

Randy blinked. "Well . . . yeah." He hadn't really expected her to leap, but he hadn't expected her to look as if someone slipped alum into her apple pie either! Scarlett's disdain rankled him and he felt compelled to mention, "Lots of women would, you know."

"I bet!" Scarlett said disbelievingly, although she knew the women of Dominion probably stood in line at Randy's door. Under different circumstances, she'd probably join them.

The medical people, viewing their exchange like it was a tennis match, held their breaths. This conversation was taking a liberal turn in a conservative atmosphere—one where some mighty sweet, generous, but old-fashioned hospital contributors might make an appearance. No one wanted to offend anyone *out* of donating funds for a new hospital wing.

During a moment of silence, Scarlett's thoughts took flight. Why did Randy have to be like all the rest? Why did he have to think *she* was like all the rest? Hot tears of humiliation clung to her lashes. "Just because I have a baby with no daddy doesn't make me a—"

"Don't!" Randy raised his free hand as soon as he realized where her sentence was leading. "Don't even say the word, Scarlett."

The people on either side of them looked anxiously at Scarlett.

"Whore." Scarlett finished her sentence, her eyes shooting jade arrows at Randy.

As the medical people groaned, Randy closed his eyes and counted to ten. He'd provoked Scarlett, he knew it. He'd not handled this with finesse. But, damn! He hated that word. He hated everything about it: the connotation behind it, the freedom with which people spewed it at others, and most of all, he hated Scarlett believing he'd think of her that way.

Opening his eyes, Randy found their immediate audience had dispersed and now leaned against the front desk, probably thinking that a safe distance.

Cowards.

Feeling Scarlett might not take him seriously with a large, colorful toy in his arms, Randy tossed the teddy bear to the orderly, then pulled the wheelchair toward him. As Scarlett tilted her head way back to look into his eyes, he told her in a low, smooth tone, "I offered to take you to my home, Scarlett, not to my bed."

Randy's soft, gentle voice washed over Scarlett, leaving her unprepared. She could deal with anger and obsession. She'd dealt with enough of that in her life! This was new to her. Take her to his home and not to his bed? Should she be flattered or offended?

He added, "If you were alone, by God, I'd probably escort you to the edge of town and say good riddance. But your baby shouldn't suffer. I went through too much with that kid to let her be turned out onto the streets."

That riled her. How dare he assume she had not considered her baby's needs! How dare he think she'd risk her baby's life! She hissed, "I wasn't going to take her out onto the streets! I was going to take a bus to a warmer climate—"

"A bus ride in your condition?!" Randy interrupted, standing up and waving his arms. "Good grief, Scarlett, did they give you bad drugs in here? Where was your mind when you conceived that plan? You'd be dead before the bus hit the next county. Where would Hank be then? Do you have some family somewhere who would raise her?"

Angry, Scarlett almost blurted out a loud "NO!" Why could he coerce her into easily revealing things she'd kept hidden for so long? She sucked her bottom lip between her teeth, seething at him, livid that he was so right! Her eyes flickered stubbornly at the orderly and nurses. "Take me to my cab, please."

They all moved in a rush, ready to wash their hands of her.

Randy informed Scarlett, "Your cab's not out there."

"What?" Scarlett shrieked, remembering just in time how painful it was to propel herself from the chair.

"I sent him away," Randy confessed.

The white-uniformed people moaned, threw up their hands, and plopped onto a few vacant chairs nearby.

Scarlett glanced at them, then glared at Randy. "You had no right to do that."

"Oh, if I see someone trying to commit suicide, I have every right to stop her." He crossed his arms.

Scarlett seethed. "I'm not *trying* to commit suicide."

"You could have fooled me." The sudden seriousness in Randy's voice stunned them both for a moment. He recovered and said, "The way I see it, you have two options. The first is you can share my apartment—"

"Get serious."

Randy choked back an unflattering comment. "Hear me out, will you?" They entered into a stare-off until Scarlett fidgeted and silently conceded to listen. Randy proceeded, "I have a small apartment over Preston's Bar and Grill in Dominion. I'm willing to share it with Hank. Since you're her mother, you're welcome to join her. It's not much, but it's better than being on the streets and you'll have a warm place to sleep—alone."

"Alone!" Scarlett scoffed.

"Alone." Randy leaned down again, this time so close his blue eyes almost mixed with her green to form a molten aquamarine pool between them. "Lady, if I wanted to get into a woman's pants, I wouldn't have to work this hard. There are a lot more agreeable pants out there to hop into, and *they* don't have the added feature of an infant!" Randy softened. "Scarlett, I'm offering you a place to stay. That's all."

"That's all?" Scarlett asked, baffled.

"There *is* one thing."

"Ah–ha!"

"When you become an able-bodied female, you pay rent."

"Oh."

Randy derived some satisfaction in knowing he had shocked her. He'd stunned her into silence. She studied him, chewing the inside of her jaw. For a moment, he thought she might accept his offer.

She asked, "What's my other option?"

Randy sighed, "*I'll* take you somewhere—a relative's home, a hotel, anywhere. *Except* a bus station or a cab."

"Like a semi is better for my health than a taxi," Scarlett returned sarcastically.

Here was the Scarlett he'd remembered. If she'd surfaced during his visit to her hospital room, he wouldn't be here now, making a fool of himself and ruining his life. He'd just be rolling out of bed after a wild night of fun and carousing . . . And Hank would be on a bus headed for the streets of a warmer city.

Randy felt a chill skip over his spine. This woman and baby were a hair's breadth away from becoming faceless statistics on some news show. "I have a pickup truck," he told her huskily.

Scarlett chewed the inside of her jaw again. There was something about the way he looked at her—as if he cared—that bothered her tremendously. She looked away, wanting to avoid his clear blue eyes and what she saw in them. She didn't know how to handle caring and concern.

What if it were all an act? What if he were luring her into a trap with those pseudo-sincere eyes of his? What if Jonas had hit upon the one true way to fool her—a man who really appeared honest and interested?

Scarlett looked up at the pink bundle in the nurse's arms. Hannah. The baby brought things down to the basics, to immediate worries. There were no what ifs in Hannah's life, only certainties. Certain hunger. Certain cold. Certain creature comforts Scarlett couldn't provide. Randy could.

He knew that, of course. He'd hit upon Scarlett's one soft, vulnerable spot, and he was using it to manipulate her. She recognized manipulation at a hundred paces, it was such a part of her life. The only question in her mind now was his motive.

Scarlett'd become a good judge of character as she'd zigzagged across the country. Her gut told her Randy knew nothing about Jonas. Her head warned her to be cautious, to remember the big picture. But what good would it do her and her baby to avoid human dangers only to die of exposure?

Scarlett would do anything for her child, including moving in with Randy for whatever reason he had in mind. At least this time she had a more noble cause for her actions.

Randy couldn't blame Scarlett for hesitating. She was running from something, something which seemed much worse than the alternative of hiking in a blizzard so close to giving birth. She had every right to be cautious. For all she knew, he could be in league with the devil.

"You'll be alone most of the time," he said, hoping to reassure her. "My truck will be ready tomorrow and I leave the next day on a short haul. After that, I hope to sign on with a broker and I will be on the road a lot. So, are you taking my offer or not?"

Scarlett's eyes flared as she looked at Randy and his heart twisted. For one brief moment, she reminded him of a rabbit he'd once cornered in a thicket. The animal's eyes reflected its turmoil of defeat and mortification. It knew its life was at the mercy of another being and the possibilities petrified it.

Randy'd freed the animal, but that wasn't the answer for Scarlett.

Scarlett shielded the emotions swirling in her eyes and said in a low, but controlled voice, "I have no alternative but to share your apartment . . . But I'll pay rent as soon as I get a job."

"Suit yourself."

The group finally left the sterile hospital environment, but even the crisp, winter air couldn't lighten the solemn atmosphere which had fallen over them. Randy knew he had to do something or the trip to Dominion would be worse than a funeral procession. Anger seemed to liven up Scarlett and he was experienced in provoking her ire.

He asked, "Did the financial aid officer come by and have you sign some papers?"

"Yes. I didn't even know you could pay—You didn't?" Randy smiled.

"You did! I don't believe you!"

"You sure are one cantankerous female!"

They argued all the way to the truck and continued even after they packed up and left the parking lot.

Scarlett fumed over Randy's interference in her life only as long as it took to reach the nearest drive-through for burgers and fries. It amazed him how a king-sized sandwich and some soggy potatoes could sweeten her disposition. He filed that information away for future reference since he'd need all the help he could get.

Scarlett ate as if she'd been starved for days, and Randy wondered if she might try to suck the grease stains from the wrappers. He noted that she didn't say one word while eating. Good ammunition, he decided. There might be a lot of *large* meals in Scarlett's future.

They rode in silence for most of the trip, commenting occasionally on some of the scenery. Although the highways were cleared of snow, the countryside was not, since the temperature had hovered around freezing for the last three days.

The closer they came to Dominion, the more civilized the area became. Farm houses, barns, and other outbuildings heavily laden with snow created a picture as lovely as any Christmas card.

"We're about five miles from Preston's," Randy told her at last. He looked at Hank who slept in the car seat between them. Except for the night Hank was born, when she inspected her world with a mild interest, Randy hadn't seen her eyes opened, nor her mouth, for that matter.

Too bad her mother couldn't follow suit.

If Scarlett wouldn't be so argumentative, she'd be an enchanting woman. Though Randy wouldn't term her a raving beauty, he found her lovely enough to aggravate his hormones. He'd taken enough cold showers to prove it.

He wondered if that would continue once he had a daily dose of her.

This feeling of being a human rope in a game of tug of war annoyed him. First, he'd get all hot and bothered over Scarlett's mane of blonde hair and those full red lips. He'd want to count every freckle on her body. Then she'd ignite like a match thrown onto dry grass and he'd want to strangle her.

He wondered if she'd be that unpredictable in bed.

Randy shook his head, ashamed of himself. The woman just had a baby, for Pete's sake! She probably had a husband, too, not that the man held much worth in Randy's book. Still, he shouldn't be having indecent thoughts about another man's wife and Hank's mother.

Preston's Bar didn't appear on the horizon one second too soon for Randy. The inside of the truck had long ago become too small for him and Scarlett. Besides, his thoughts warmed the small space to an uncomfortable level.

The bar, a large warehouse-size wooden structure, was built to resemble a western-style saloon. The ornate filigree trim, the bright sign professing the name, and a long hitching post out front succeeded in giving it the effect Preston sought.

It was the hub of entertainment for miles and miles, offering a band during the weekend, a DJ on weeknights, and the best food and drink on the Carolina coast. As a result, Preston and his wife, Marie, enjoyed a cushy life.

Changing very little since the doors first opened, Preston's Bar offered continuity to its customers. The food was still the best, the service personable, and the entertainment lively. Preston and Marie had picked up some gray hair and wrinkles over the years, but they were still the same good people everyone knew and loved and came back to see.

This time of the day—after the lunch crunch and before the happy-hour rush—only Preston's gray 4 X 4 and a red Camaro owned by one of the employees sat out front. In a few hours even the back parking lot would be full of cars.

Randy parked around back where a set of steps led to a second floor landing and a door.

"We're home!" Randy announced to Scarlett as he jumped from the truck and came around to open her door.

Scarlett ran an appraising stare over each step to the apartment. She grimaced.

"If you can't make it, I'll carry you," Randy said, lightly. "You *have* to be lighter than the last time I carried you."

Scarlett stuck out her tongue at him, then released an uncharacteristic laugh.

Randy stood motionless as the sound washed over him. He couldn't recall her laughing before, although in their brief association, she'd had very little reason to break out in a good guffaw. She'd smiled, but he had never been blessed with such a pleasant sound coming from her mouth, he was sure of that. He'd just have to figure out a way to make this a regular event.

Scarlett unstrapped Hank and lifted her from the infant chair as if she held a porcelain doll—beautiful to look at, but easily broken with the slightest misplaced touch.

Randy suspected that Scarlett knew no more about babies than he did. Poor Hank!

Scarlett managed the stairs very well. Randy followed close behind her, ready to assist should she need it. By the time he'd unlocked and opened the door, she aimed for the nearest piece of furniture.

A worn recliner sat five feet from the door and Scarlett dropped onto it, a grateful smile on her lips.

Scarlett held Hank close to her as she caught her breath

and took in the details of her new home—the home she now shared with Randy. She glanced up at him with a nervous shiver, then continued her survey of the apartment.

It was a mixture of early mobile home and late Salvation Army furniture, but amazingly tidy for a confirmed bachelor's pad.

They stood in one long, narrow room with a large window near the outside door. Beside the recliner sat a low table, with nothing on top except a remote control aimed at the console television against the wall straight ahead. A brown-and-green plaid sofa, worn but comfortable looking, was to her left with a small table butted against one end.

The table was the only cluttered area of the whole room. Piled up under a heavy dark-green lamp were trucking magazines . . . and *art* magazines. Could those be Randy's? No.

Scarlett conjured up a vision of Randy eagerly flipping through the pages of the newest art magazine while chugging a beer. She could see him toss the periodical aside in anger because not one good likeness of Elvis captured on black velvet appeared between its covers. Art magazines? Randy? The two didn't mesh, but then he'd been Mr. Full-of-Surprises ever since she met him, she reminded herself.

His dining room reminded Scarlett of the fifties. An aluminum table with four red plastic upholstered chairs sat beneath the window. A set of diner-style salt and pepper shakers, as well as a terra cotta dish holding two thriving cacti adorned the table.

The kitchen took up the entire back wall, consisting of ample counter space separating the full-size refrigerator from the stove. In the very middle was a double sink. Above, open shelves held Randy's collection of dishes and canned goods.

The remaining wall was interior and contained two

doors. Scarlett assumed one of them led to the bathroom and the other led to the bedroom. *One* bedroom.

Scarlett's gaze hit Randy like a green cobra ready to strike. Mr. Full-of-Surprises had only *one* bedroom! She watched him saunter over to the refrigerator and rummage through it. She was about to confront him over the sleeping arrangements when he called to her, "The sofa's a sleeper. You and Hank can have the bedroom since I'll be getting up early a lot."

Scarlett's mouth clamped shut. He was giving up his bed for her and her daughter? She eyed the old sofa. It couldn't be comfortable. She looked back at Mr. Full-of-Surprises.

Randy was the most unusual man she'd ever met. He was just plain nice and it scared the hell out of her. At least the others had given her an insight into their true nature so she hadn't been completely taken off-guard when they turned on her. Randy was the type of man who didn't chip away at mental walls—he demolished them.

He could demolish some other walls, too.

She watched with more pleasure than she should as the taut muscles of his legs stretched beneath the soft fabric of his jeans. He leaned down and seized the neck of an orange juice bottle, biceps bunching against the sleeves of his red pullover shirt.

"Want some jui—" Randy stopped in mid-sentence when he caught the odd way she regarded him. *Good Lord, she's not going to cry, is she?* "Juice?"

Scarlett shook her head.

"Are you all right?" he asked, not sure he wanted to deal with what was wrong. He poured himself a glass of orange juice, wishing there was a good belt of Vodka in it.

"Oh, I'm fine. I just feel I owe you an apology and a thank you."

Randy's head shot up in surprise and he stared at her.

"Your juice is going to overflow," Scarlett warned him.

Damned right it was if she kept looking at him like that! Her eyes lowered to his hands and he realized she meant *orange* juice. He righted the bottle just before the liquid reached the top of the glass. He took a big gulp to make it more manageable, but mostly to wet his dry throat.

Scarlett stared at Hannah a long time before she explained. When she spoke, her voice was low and husky. "You see, I can't seem to do anything right when you are around.

She smiled. "I didn't decide at the beginning of the week that my goals were to be in a truck that ran off the road, nearly get killed, have a stranger deliver my baby in that truck, and then move in with the stranger."

Randy remained silent.

Scarlett looked at him, her expression serious, her eyes filled with gratitude. "And I *sure* didn't plan for the stranger to be so damned nice."

"Just call me a good samaritan." Randy took another gulp from his glass.

"You are either a saint or I'm going to have one large tab to pay one of these days," she said, hoping he understood she was referring to paying him back in bed.

"I'm no saint, Scarlett, and I told you the only payment I expect is help with the household expenses."

She wanted to believe that. She wanted to hold onto that one thread of hope that a decent human being still existed, but how could she expect it of someone else when she wasn't decent herself? She expelled a shaky breath. "I can't remember the last time someone was nice to me and didn't hand me a price tag at the same time. It must have been before I was six. That was when my mother died."

So, her mother's dead. Randy couldn't say he knew

how it felt to lose a parent, but he knew what it was like to be small and have no one.

He noted the quivering twist of Scarlett's lips as she struggled to keep them still. Her voice was low and raspier than normal. What had this woman been through? Even *he'd* tasted the milk of human kindness—often. He'd known unconditional generosity and had benefitted from such occurrences in his life. He extended help to others in need whenever the occasion arose.

To Randy, kindness was like the pennies in those dishes storekeepers kept on their counters. "Need a penny?" the sign beside the cash register read, "Take one. Got a penny? Give one."

Scarlett had never been allowed to dip her hand into the kindness jar without leaving something in return. It made her a mighty angry, defensive young woman. Could he blame her? What payment came due with each kindness she'd been offered? And who had handed her the bills?

His heartbeat accelerated as his imagination conjured up a list of horrible answers to his questions.

Scarlett forced a lighter tone into her voice. "It's just a hard thing for me to believe, and an even harder thing for me to accept, that someone is nice to me—even though I *am* a bitch."

Randy's heart flung itself against his chest cavity as she gave him that Mona Lisa smile. It didn't make him feel as if he'd done something stupid as usual. This time it shot primitive lust through him like mercury through a hot thermometer.

Scarlett's lashes fluttered over her almond-shaped eyes.

Randy felt done-in. He felt roped and dragged right into the glorious depths of those green eyes. He might as well be falling into a lake of ignited gasoline—both were equally dangerous.

Hank saved him. She awoke, found herself in a strange environment with no recollection of getting there, and voiced her protest. This came in a small meowing sound at first, followed by a series of "ka-ha's," which turned into glass-breaking "wah's."

"What the hell's wrong with her?" Randy asked, alarmed.

"It's called crying," Scarlett told him exasperatedly.

"Damn!" Randy shook his head as Hank's cries began resounding at the bottom vertebrae of his spine and worked their way up, stopping at each bone to give it a good vibration. Hank's beet-red face twisted and wrinkled with the effort. Her eyes scrunched together and her mouth stretched to its capacity. *Now*, she favored her mother.

"What will stop her?" he asked, hoping for a miracle cure.

"How should I know?" Scarlett rocked Hank and patted her diapered bottom.

"You don't know?"

Scarlett shook her head.

"I thought you women were born knowing these things."

Scarlett gave him a level gaze. "Cut the sexist remarks and find something for a crib."

"A crib? We forgot a bed for the kid?" Randy asked. "I can't believe this!"

Five minutes later, after considering all the possibilities and muttering under his breath, Randy tossed the contents of his sock drawer into a remote corner of his bedroom. He lined the drawer with an old sweater, then covered it with a pillowcase and re-entered the living room. Holding his creation up for Scarlett's approval, he said, "You know, Scarlett, we're a real pair. For Hank's sake we should pin a note on her diaper and leave her on a doorstep somewhere."

Scarlett glared at him. He shrugged and placed the "crib" on the table.

"I think she's hungry," Scarlett announced.

"Do we have bottles?" he asked, glancing at the pink bag she brought from the hospital.

"Ah . . ."

"No bottles either?" Randy rested his hands on his hips. "I'll get a pen and paper for that note."

"There are . . . adequate containers."

"What does that mean?"

"I'm breast-feeding her," she said as nonchalantly as if she was telling him the state of the weather.

Randy couldn't help it, his eyes fell to the swell of breast beneath that unbecoming black coat. A blush crept up from the collar of his red shirt and inched toward his hairline.

"It's cheaper," Scarlett explained with a shrug.

Randy's eyes lifted to hers, catching the amused green sparkle around her dark pupils and the twitch of her lips itching to curve into a smile.

Scarlett couldn't believe he was so easily embarrassed! She'd found his delivering Hannah a bit unnerving and still felt uncomfortable about his knowledge of her anatomy, but he was the Casanova of the Open Road. Breast feeding shouldn't produce such a flaming flush to his skin! She felt compelled to deepen the color. "No bottles to wash. No formula to heat. Just unbutton the blouse—"

"I get the picture, Scarlett!" he interrupted then heaved a sigh. "I'm going to Preston's for a beer. You'll have complete privacy."

As he stalked passed her aiming for the door, he saluted Hank and mumbled, "*Bon appetit.*"

Preston Davis, standing behind the mirrored and brass-trimmed bar, spotted Randy when he cleared the back door. He reached into the ice box and extended a beer over the polished surface. "You look like you could use this, boy."

Randy took it, nodded in gratitude, and uncapped the bottle with an impatient flick of his wrist. Tipping back his head, he took a long chug of the golden liquid and smacked his lips in approval. He said, "Thanks, there's nothing like an ice cold one to put you in a better mood."

Preston leaned on the bar and smiled. "I guess that means they're all moved in."

Randy nodded. "Are they ever!"

He'd discussed his plans with Preston and Marie when he first thought of sharing the apartment. After all, the place did belong to the Davises. He also valued their opinion. When Randy first moved into the area, he couldn't believe his luck at finding the apartment. It was such a reasonable rent, he almost broke the sound barrier getting to it before someone else beat him out of a great deal. During that time, he'd thrown every spare penny into his truck fund and didn't have a lot of extra cash. Besides, all he wanted was a place to store his belongings and somewhere to sleep when he wasn't on the road. Being so near a bar didn't hurt either.

Preston and Marie were a priceless bonus. They were the loving, happy people with strong values and senses of humor he'd always wanted for parents. He was the son— the child—they could never have.

"Scarlett's *breast-feeding* Hank now. I got out of there."

Preston choked back a laugh. "It *is* a natural act, Randy."

Randy's eyes flashed at him. "Oh, yeah? They say childbirth is natural, too . . . It's not."

Preston nodded, then raised an eyebrow. "Hey, I thought you said the baby is a girl."

"She is."

"And her name is Hank?"

"Her name is Hannah."

"But you call her Hank?"

"It's better than Hannah."

Preston rolled his eyes and straightened, grabbing a glass to polish. "O–kay. Glad that's cleared up."

Randy groaned. "What have I gotten myself into?"

"I've been wondering that myself."

"Why didn't you say something to me when I brought this up?" Randy asked, wishing Preston had dished out some fatherly advice when Randy'd decided to take on a roommate.

"You're a big boy."

Randy rolled the beer bottle between his hands and studied it for a moment. He didn't feel like a big boy. Right now, he felt like a stupid adolescent—one with some serious growing pains.

"Is this beer on the house?" Randy asked. "I might have to buy diapers tonight."

Preston threw back his head and had a good belly laugh. "Wait 'til I tell Marie about this! Yeah, the beer's on the house. And so is a steak dinner for you and the lady who can get you to buy diapers!"

Two beers later, Randy left the bar. The regulars would soon be arriving and he didn't want to be talked into staying nor did he feel like explaining why he couldn't.

Upstairs, only the low murmur of the television disturbed the quiet of the apartment. Hank, fed and satisfied, slumbered in her drawer, which now sat on the floor near the sofa. The dying afternoon sun made a last stab through the window and spotlighted Scarlett lying on the couch.

Randy heaved a ragged breath as he beheld Scarlett. The sunlight wasn't even strong enough to worry her from her sleep. Curled on her side, her hands tucked beneath her cheek, she looked as sweet as her baby.

Randy crossed the room, snatching the multi-colored afghan from his chair as he passed. Leaning down, he draped the crocheted square over Scarlett as she moved in her sleep.

She spoke.

At least he thought she did. He waited.

She sighed and in what sounded to him like the whisper of a love-satisfied woman, she murmured two words.

"Oh, Jonas."

FIVE

Randy dropped onto the recliner, his energy suddenly evaporated.

Jonas.

Damn! Just hearing the man's name made him as weak as a newborn colt! Or . . . maybe it was the *way* Scarlett said it that stunned Randy so much. Hell! It was as if she still *loved* the guy! After he deserted her? Deserted Hank!

Even Scarlett should have more intelligence than that! Disgusted, Randy looked away, fixing his eyes on a point somewhere above the TV.

What if Jonas didn't desert them? What if he's dead?

Randy's eyes pivoted to Scarlett as this new revelation hit him.

A dead man's memory is damned hard to compete with.

"Where the *hell* did that come from?" Randy rocketed from the chair, then quickly inspected the couch and drawer. Neither female had been roused by his outburst.

He raked a nervous hand through the curls at the nape of his neck. He wasn't about to compete with any man—living or dead—for Scarlett, or any woman for that matter. Never had and wasn't about to start now.

Randy was a lover, not a fighter. He loved all women

in general and none in particular. Finding something worthwhile in every female gave him unlimited options. Why spar for *one* lady's affections when another just as intelligent, fascinating, and lovely waited around the next corner?

But was there another one with the same combination of freckle-spattered porcelain skin, peach-dusted cheeks, and an aurora of burnished gold surrounding her head and shoulders?

"Damned right there is!" Randy bellowed, this time not checking to see if he disturbed the women and not caring if he did. He began to pace the small space between the chair and the door.

Okay, he wasn't the Casanova Dominion thought him to be. Randy had always been a sexually responsible person, even before the AIDS scare, and he dated very little, actually. It was just that the good citizens never saw him with the same lady twice, and that spelled promiscuity to them.

But even though he wasn't the Romeo of the Open Road, as Dixie preferred to call him, he was *not* a one-woman man.

He looked at Scarlett again, following the curved profile of her body beneath the afghan. The softly rounded shoulder, the peak of her hip, and the not-too-short-not-too-long legs all appealed to everything male within him.

Could I compete?

Would I lose?

Randy whirled around and headed for the kitchen. "This is way *too* serious to even consider!"

He yanked open the refrigerator door, hoping to God there was a beer inside.

There wasn't.

He slammed the door and leaned against the refrigerator in frustration. This frustration was from the absence of beer, he assured himself.

No, Randy conceded—*this* frustration was the uncomfortable tightness in his jeans.

Groaning, he stomped toward the bathroom, stripping off his shirt. ''These cold showers are getting *pretty* old!''

Scarlett took the coconut shell filled with a sweet potable, slices of fruit, and a colorful umbrella. The sun beat down upon her. Its rays bounced gloriously off the white sand beneath her bare feet, catching every facet of the diamond tennis bracelet around her slender wrist. It was one of many birthday presents from Jonas.

She smiled up at Jonas and found him smiling back. She loved the way he looked. The deep, brown eyes. The distinguished gray of his hair. She loved the way he kept himself in shape when other men his age were letting themselves go.

They were suddenly in a cave along the beach. Jonas was removing her wrap-around skirt and spreading it on the damp sand. He pushed her down upon it and followed her. Mint green bikini and navy designer shorts were tossed into a heap together. The sounds of waves crashing against the rocks filled her ears as Jonas filled her body.

''Oh, Jonas . . .''

Scarlett was chained to the wall of the cave. Through the semi-darkness, she could see guards all about her. By her side, in front of her, at the cave entrance.

She could hear Jonas laughing. It was a cruel, sinister sound—the sound of someone enjoying another's misfortune. She realized his laugh had always sounded like that. He'd always been on the border of insanity.

She struggled against the shackles, but could move no more than her head. Jonas snickered.

He stepped into the pool of light before her and she cringed at the sight of his twisted features.

''I'll take the baby, Scarlett,'' he hissed.

Her eyes dropped to the rounded bulge of her stomach. *Pregnant?*

"I can do it," he said, his voice bringing her terrified, confused gaze back up to his eyes.

She was an animal snared in a trap with the hunter coming toward her.

"I have the money and the power. I can take the baby, Scarlett, and there's not a damned thing you can do about it."

"No—o—o!" Scarlett's head shook from side to side. Her eyes closed in the pain of reality—the man she once thought of as loving and giving was trying to hurt her in the worst possible way. His face was close to hers now, breathing the air meant for *her* lungs.

"I can do it, Scarlett. I can do it, Scarlett. I can do it, Scarlett."

As Jonas repeated the words over and over, Scarlett began to sob. She closed her eyes as he gripped her shoulders and began to shake her . . .

"Scarlett. Scarlett, wake up."

Her eyes popped open and she raised her hands in a defensive movement. Her heart pounded so loudly she could hear only its deafening throb above her ragged intake of breath.

Scarlett froze in fear, disoriented and confused. She recognized the man whose brow creased with concern, but for a moment, she thought it was Jonas in disguise. For a moment she was still afraid.

One thought seeped into Scarlett's mind above the fear for her own life and her disappointment with Jonas. One thought ripped through everything else. *The baby*!

Scarlett bolted upright, shaking off the man's hand. Dread lumped in her throat as her trembling fingers inched over her stomach. Horror filled her eyes as she forced herself to look down.

Flat!

Her stomach was flat!

Shakily, Scarlett's hands plowed through her disheveled hair as a real scream threatened to erupt from her. Frantic, she glanced about at her surroundings. Panic strangled her lungs. Tears stung her eyes. Her thoughts were mired in fear.

"Scarlett!" Randy gripped her arms and forced her to look at him. "You were having a nightmare! Come out of it!"

Scarlett focused for the first time. Like a curtain lifting over a window, her mind cleared. She looked down at the spot where she left Hannah and a joyful cry escaped her. The baby rested peacefully in the drawer, her tiny hands balled into fists and her mouth puckered.

Scarlett plucked her child from the makeshift crib and held her close. Hannah tolerated the nuzzling and cuddling and fussing with a scrunched face and squinted eyes.

Things were beginning to come back to Scarlett now. Like the pain in her lower body which reminded her of Hannah's birth three days ago.

It had all been a nightmare—like the others over the last few months, but more frightening—and Jonas was not here at all. "It *was* a nightmare," she exclaimed as she lay Hannah against her shoulder and hugged her again.

"A nightmare," Randy repeated, crossing his arms and scowling at her.

Scarlett looked up at him. *Oh, yeah. Randy.*

Even with the frown marring his otherwise gentle features, he was appealing.

That was her problem. Everything about him was *too* appealing.

In such a short time, Randy was much more important to her than he should be. That scared her.

In the past seven months, Scarlett paid for help. The sweat of her brow got her a job. Picking melons got her a place to sleep. A few dollars got her a hot meal. Although she'd *paid* for that help, Jonas punished those people for getting her one step further away from him.

Scarlett felt guilty when she discovered this, of course,

but she had her baby to think about . . . She had herself to think about, she admitted, even if it might seem ruthless.

The guilt had never lasted long.

But she knew that wouldn't be the case if Jonas harmed Randy in any way for helping her. She'd leave as soon as she was able. Maybe Jonas would never find out about him. Maybe she'd be lucky.

After all, she'd been practically Jonas-free since she hopped from Utah to Canada and then here to North Carolina. It completely blitzed her established pattern. Of course, it had also completely blitzed her money reserves, but two weeks of only memories and bad dreams to haunt her had been worth every penny. Maybe it would last.

Who was she kidding? Jonas would find her. He probably already knew where she was. She had to leave soon. If Randy suffered because of being kind to her, she'd . . . Well, she wouldn't get over the guilt very fast.

"Do you *always* wake up like Freddy Krueger's chasing you?" Randy questioned, his tone interlaced with worry.

"No," she said, "sometimes it's Jason." She offered him a smile.

He didn't return it.

Scarlett sighed. Humor was never her forté.

His concern touched her, however.

Randy stalked into the kitchen, grabbed a glass from the cabinet, and yanked open the refrigerator. He filled the glass with orange juice and drained it dry.

Damn! Either all this juice was eating through his stomach or this woman had already given him an ulcer!

He slammed the glass onto the counter a bit too hard and for a moment expected to feel fragments of it in his hand.

Scarlett prompted the widest range of emotions in him any mortal ever had. And his feelings were constantly changing! One second, he was under a cold shower trying to tame his tempted male hormones. The next moment, he wanted to rip out the liver of whoever caused her to wake up sweating and frenzied. Right now, he was torn between shaking her until she confided in him and holding her until she did. Damnit! Hadn't he proved he could be trusted?

"Randy—"

"Scarlett—"

They stopped and eyed each other. She saw questions. He saw a plea not to ask them.

Okay. For right now, he'd let the questions lie.

"Preston invited us to eat at the bar tonight if you're up to it."

Scarlett sagged with relief, then nodded, her enthusiasm bubbling to the surface. "Up to it? I'm famished!"

Randy turned to the sink and ran water into the glass. "The bathroom's free. I've taken my shower."

And changed your clothes. She ran an appraising gaze over him.

While she was asleep, he'd changed into a charcoal gray sweatsuit which skimmed over every angle of his lean form, leaving very little of his body to the imagination. Her eyes followed the ripple of muscle tissue along his shoulders and across his back. She noted the way the soft fabric caressed his taut backside like a pair of feminine hands. She could almost feel the smooth skin, the squared derriere, and the point where thigh met hip.

He turned around.

Her eyes dropped to the floor and an erotic tremor tap danced across the pit of her stomach as she spied Randy's bare feet. She'd never considered herself having a foot fetish before, but his well-defined arches and sexy toes brought out latent tendencies.

"Something wrong with my feet?" Randy asked defensively.

Scarlett's eyes shot upward. "Nope! Nothing's wrong!"

He eyed her warily.

Clearing her throat, Scarlett replaced Hannah in the

crib, lifted the drawer, and hurried for the bathroom. "I think I'll see if Hannah is hungry and then take a shower."

Randy waited long enough for the door to close, then he leaned against the counter for a moment.

Beets! He'd thought of those damned ugly, purple vegetables! He concentrated on the one food that most disgusted him to keep his private anatomy from going public. The brief moment before Scarlett shielded her emotions, he'd caught the volatile heat and hunger in her eyes. It aroused him and teased him.

He walked stiff legged to the bedroom to dress for the evening.

He needed a woman.

Preston's was lively by the time they entered. A sea of blue jeans and cowboy hats filled the space from the door to the dance floor. Men and women huddled together in whispered conversations or eyed each other in long-distance lust.

Through the cloud of smoke above the clientele's heads a stage was visible, vacant except for shiny instruments and elaborate sound equipment. The music, loud enough to hear over the laughter and talking, came from a source other than a band.

The bouncer, who waived the cover charge at the door, cast an inquisitive glance at Scarlett and Hank. Randy never explained the woman and infant, though Tony kept him engaged in small talk for a good five minutes.

The bouncer wasn't the only curious one. As they pushed through the crowd gathered at the door and entered the clearing near the bar, most eyes were upon them.

"Hey, Randy," a buxom blonde posing at the end of the bar greeted him, then tossed a glare at Scarlett.

"Hey, Crystal," Randy said.

A few men called to him and he returned a nod or a word of greeting. Everyone else didn't bother to hide his astonishment or, as in the case of some hopeful ladies, disappointment. Randy, the womanizer and child hater, was bringing both *into* the bar!

Randy wasn't taking this as calmly as he appeared. Although used to getting attention, he wasn't keen on being the center of it. Nor did he like his reputation as a lady's man being damaged. Especially not tonight.

He needed some male-female interaction. Bad. Scarlett was getting to his sexual senses, a sure sign he'd been too long without a woman.

Even though Scarlett appeared just as agitated and willing as he was, it was technically impossible right now. He'd heard it took six weeks for a woman to mend after childbirth. He'd never wait six weeks! He'd be a mass of twisted nerves by then!

Besides, he didn't think it was a good idea for them to become sexually involved. He'd never cohabitated with a sexual interest before. His reaction to "Jonas" told him he'd already gotten a bit too emotionally involved. Mixing sex and emotional involvement was not a smart thing to do. Ever.

Judging from the looks on the faces of his usual contacts, he'd have to do a lot of smooth talking to take one of these ladies home tonight.

"Hey, Taylor!"

The shout pulled Randy from his thoughts to the bar where a beer-bellied chunk of humanity perched on a barstool. His eyes ran over the man's face, which was just a blob with two spots for eyes and a curved gash serving as a mouth. His gaze fell to the Jack Daniels T-shirt stretched thin over the man's rotund stomach and then to the pudgy hand wrapped around a can of Milwaukee's best. Randy lifted his eyes to stare at the man and waited. He'd let this side of beef call the shots.

Scarlett could tell that whatever this good-ol'-boy was about to say would send them down the trail of no good. His smirk and the sarcastic way he got Randy's attention gave her a sense of dread. The last thing she needed was for someone to tease her out of Randy's house and home.

Scarlett silently appealed to the man to just shut up.

"That kid looks like you!" Beer-belly, feeling proud of himself for initiating a round of laughter from those sitting near him, slapped his knee and guffawed. The sound, vibrating from the depths of his vast midsection, was a cross between a snort and an oink.

Befitting, Scarlett thought.

She and Randy studied Hannah for a minute or two.

Well, come to think of it, she did look a little like Randy, although right now she mainly resembled Yoda from *Star Wars*. She did have curly chestnut hair and a lot of it, just like Randy. Her eyes were a darker shade of blue, but there was not a hint of green in them. And, to Scarlett's chagrin, she possessed a dark complexion like Randy.

Scarlett met Randy's eyes. What was he thinking? It was a mistake to bring the kid in here? He was going to fight Beer-Belly for insulting him? She couldn't tell and fear wiggled along her spine.

Randy turned back to Beer-Belly and said, jovially, "Well, Dave, the way I look at it, she's lucky. She *could* look like you."

Dave's friends howled at him, causing his face to become redder, if that was possible. He lifted from the barstool and Scarlett looked about for escape or help.

Dave's friends looked ready and able to back him should there be a fight. Hell, Dave already outweighed Randy by a good hundred pounds. Alone he could probably damage Randy for life! If he let him live, that is.

And there was Randy, eyes like cold steel and standing his ground. Didn't he realize the only ones on his side were a post-partum woman and a six-pound infant? Men and their machismo!

Scarlett sucked in a deep breath and sent up a silent

prayer for there to be no fight—especially not because of her.

Dave's buddies reached for him and lowered him back to the stool.

"Let it go, Dave," one said. "Hell, you're the one who started it."

Randy waited long enough to make sure Dave took his friends' advice then he moved Scarlett in front of him and proceeded through the bar turned gauntlet.

Stunned, Scarlett walked in silence.

Aside from the fact that Randy hadn't denied Hannah was his, he impressed Scarlett with the way he handled himself. He hadn't asked for trouble, but he'd not run away. He'd not even shown fear. He was presenting himself as a much more honorable man than she figured. What an enigma!

"Let me see that precious bundle!"

Randy recognized the voice. Scarlett didn't and she pulled Hank close to her as a tall, slender woman trotted toward her, arms spread wide.

"It's okay," Randy said close to Scarlett's ear. "She's Preston's wife, Marie."

Something about the woman's warm, brown eyes and pleasant face made Scarlett relinquish her daughter to the stranger.

"Oh, she's beautiful!" Marie smiled down at Hank.

Randy couldn't see it himself. Hank was cute if you liked a wrinkled, splotchy miniature human. But beautiful? Nah.

"You'd think she never saw a baby before," Preston said as he joined them and handed Randy a beer.

Randy felt like grabbing it with both hands, his nerves were so stripped. The cap already off, he only had to lift it to his lips and chug. Which he did. "Thanks, Preston."

Scarlett looked at the slightly gray-haired man. A few distinguished lines about his sparkling blue eyes and a little-boy grin gave him a mischievous appeal which reminded her of Randy.

Randy introduced them, "Scarlett, this is Preston Davis and his wife, Marie. And this is Scarlett Kincaid and Hank—my roomies."

Scarlett felt as if she were meeting Randy's parents as they exchanged handshakes and greetings.

"Oh, can I take her off your hands while you eat?" Marie asked, her face bright with anticipation.

Scarlett hesitated only a moment before she nodded. The idea of eating in peace sounded good to her. She loved Hannah with all her heart and wasn't sorry she had her, but motherhood was something she'd been ill-prepared for. A break would be nice.

"You may not see her for days," Preston commented as he watched his wife disappear into the crowd with Hannah. Turning back to Scarlett, he said, "I hope you're comfortable in the apartment. It wasn't built for roomies and an infant. It was built for lovers."

Randy choked on his beer and eyed Preston. *What's he up to?*

Preston ignored him. "It's where me and Marie lived when we were first married."

Scarlett smiled. His grin made her wish those walls could talk.

"Well," Preston glanced at Randy, "I guess you'd like your table."

Randy didn't have to be told twice to follow Preston. He dogged the older man's footsteps as he led them down two steps toward the dance floor and stopped at an empty table with a RESERVED sign on it.

Randy stared at the table then checked its position for visibility. Everyone in the bar could see them.

"Well, hell, Preston, why didn't you just put us on the stage?" he asked, flustered.

Preston shoved his hands into the pockets of his jeans and shrugged. "Sorry. I knew nothing about it until it was too late. Marie reserved the table while I was taking care of a problem in the kitchen. By the time I saw it, the other tables were full.''

''Randy, if this is a problem, we don't have to stay. I'm really not that hungry.'' Scarlett's voice trembled.

Randy liked it better when she was screaming and hissing at him. At least then she wasn't appealing to his senses in every possible way.

He looked at her and sighed. Her eyes were like green glass. She'd sucked her bottom lip between her teeth—no doubt to keep it from quivering.

What was wrong with him anyway? He'd been the pawn of a matchmaking game before and it never bothered him. He'd laughed it off good-naturedly. At least this one was so obvious he didn't have to work to figure it out.

Besides, he shouldn't take his frustrations out on Scarlett.

''No, Scarlett, you *are* hungry and so am I. And I'm not one to pass up a free meal.''

She relaxed when he smiled, his deep dimples creasing his freshly shaved cheeks.

The twenty minutes before the salad arrived were the worst for Randy. He had nothing to do except fidget under everyone's scrutinizing stares and watch his unlimited options dwindle to slim pickings as the single ladies began to pair up with the available men. He added two more beers to the earlier ones.

By the time the waitress set their entrees before them, he'd relaxed a lot. He wasn't sure if it was because the novelty wore off and people lost interest or because the buzz resulting from beer on an empty stomach gave him a real attitude adjustment.

The aroma of steak and fries caused his stomach to growl and rumble. He ate a strip of fried potato to satisfy the emptiness until he could administer all the proper sauces and condiments necessary for proper eating.

Scarlett had remained amazingly quiet and still until this

point. She watched the goings on about her, which were always interesting in Preston's. She gave Randy space, sensing his desire not to talk.

Now, however, she leaned forward, sniffed her food and cut a square of steak. Popping it into her mouth, she moaned with a pleasure Randy didn't need to hear right now. "This is so—o—o good!"

Randy got the feeling it had been awhile since she had a real good meal. "You haven't tasted mine yet."

"You cook?" Her eyes lifted in surprise.

"Honey, I am a gourmet." He grabbed a roll from the basket near his left hand, pulled it apart, then began to butter it.

"Did your mother or father teach you?"

"Neither."

Randy bit off a corner of the hot roll, relishing the flavor of the rich, melted butter.

He chewed and swallowed, then noticed her silence. When he met her almond eyes, he saw mild curiosity.

"The people at the home taught me."

"The . . . home?"

Scarlett's eyes ignited with a bit of fear and at least a hundred questions. Her mouth even opened to verbalize those questions, then clamped shut. She was going to offer him the same respect for privacy he'd given her.

He considered letting her stay in the dark, but even though he thought she was a little crazy it wasn't fair to let *her* think she stepped into *One Flew Over the Cuckoo's Nest*.

He made himself clearer, "The *Children's* Home, Houston, Texas."

"A—An orphanage?" Scarlett rested her fork on her plate. "Randy, you grew up in an orphanage?"

Her concern made him happy and uncomfortable at the same time. "Oh, don't look so sad. It wasn't that bad. They taught me to cook." He flashed her his most beguiling grin.

Scarlett's smile was a bad imitation of his. She was hiding sadness, maybe even pity. He wouldn't tolerate pity from anyone. Randy lay down his fork and knife. "I didn't know any life except the orphanage, Scarlett. When you've never known any different, it's not so bad," he told her honestly, although he didn't know why he'd said anything in the first place.

Only Preston and Marie knew all the details of how he grew up. He wasn't ashamed of it—he'd done nothing wrong—but he didn't like being on sympathy's receiving end.

What he saw in Scarlett's eyes right now was not sympathy nor pity, but he couldn't find a name for it, either. He just knew what he saw made him feel all warm inside.

"You were never adopted?" Scarlett asked, her tone teetering somewhere between not wanting to pry and afraid she'd hit the wrong nerve.

He shook his head. "I had asthma from the time I was born until I was six. It was so bad, I could hardly ever go outside. I got a lot of special attention from the employees at the home for that reason. But no one wants to adopt a sick child."

"But you seem perfectly healthy to me." She allowed a gaze to wander over the line of his shoulders working against the brown suede fabric of his jacket as he cut his steak. She caught a glimpse of cinnamon chest hairs peeking above the vee of his crisp white shirt and tried to guess if that was the sum total, or if he'd be hairy from collar bone to belly button. She knew beneath the heavily varnished table were a pair of tight black jeans encasing perfectly healthy legs. *Yessir. Mighty healthy!*

Scarlett cleared her throat. "I mean, I'd never know you have asthma."

"I don't. I had a case of whooping cough when I was six. The doctor said if it didn't kill me, it would cure me. He didn't expect me to live."

Randy's lips curved and his electric eyes seemed recharged as he looked at her. "But, as you see, I did. The whooping cough meant to kill me cured my asthma."

"Amazing."

"Everyone thought so." He paused long enough to devour another fry and some steak then told her, "But I was not a baby any longer."

"And no one wants to adopt an older kid."

"Exactly."

"Oh."

Randy lifted his eyes, stopping his movements in the middle of slicing off another mouthful of steak. "Scarlett, don't look so dismal. *I'm* not dismal. I had a lot of people who cared a lot about me. Coaches, teachers, friends, the people at the home. A lot of kids don't have that. Family isn't determined by blood or formed by a set of legal papers."

Scarlett thought of her own situation and couldn't agree with him more. Blood relatives had done nothing but fail her, and legalities only threatened her life and Hannah's happiness.

Randy added, "I think I turned out pretty good."

"I'll say!"

His brow raised.

She didn't notice. "I can't imagine why no one adopted you—baby or not! Everyone loves you. You're so outgoing and friendly. And normal! Look at me, and *I* grew up with my father."

Randy laughed. "Oh, you're not so bad. A bit deranged, maybe, and I don't think I'll let you near my semi again, but you're all right."

That wasn't exactly true. The deranged part was true. The part about never letting her near his semi again was up for debate. With her hair pulled up on each side of her face, some of it cascading across her right shoulder and her green sweater deepening her eyes to emerald, she was much more than all right. She maybe could talk him into anything.

Randy scanned the bar once more for available women.
"My goodness! Was that a compliment?"

Randy's attentions centered on Scarlett again. She'd
placed a hand over her heart in falsetto surprise.

He blinked in mock amazement, going along with her
unusually light disposition. "By George, I believe it
was!"

Scarlett laughed. Though not loud, Randy heard it
above the chaos surrounding them. On a serious note, he
said, "You should laugh more often."

She shrugged. "I haven't had a lot to laugh about
lately."

Scarlett's head bowed and she pushed around the fries
and piece of steak on her plate with her fork.

Randy leaned back in his chair and studied her. She'd
gone quiet on him and he feared the next step was tears.
He had two courses of action as he saw it. He could
pursue her depression and possibly bring out the answers
to all his questions. Or he could try to pull her out of her
doldrums.

He chose the latter since they were in a public place.
The last thing he needed was for her to cry as she satisfied
his curiosity and turn his Don Juan image into Marquis de
Sade.

"Well, that was a good meal. Want some dessert?"

Scarlett's head jerked up. "Are you serious? I shouldn't
have eaten this. I still have about fifteen more pounds to
lose."

Randy didn't think so. Those fifteen pounds gave her a
womanly softness that appealed to his masculine senses.
He wanted to explore every rounded inch of her. "You
don't need to lose weight."

Scarlett merely stared at him.

He leaned on the table and smiled. "Now, which do
you want—apple pie or chocolate cake? They're the best."

Scarlett surrendered. "Apple pie. Are you going to be

on the road very much? If not, I'll get so big, I'll break the stairs to the apartment!"

Later, as they pushed the emptied dessert plates aside, Preston came to the table. "Well, folks, how was it?"

"Delicious!" Scarlett announced, beaming up at Preston. "But I'm going to have to exercise twice as much tomorrow."

Preston waved his hand. "A slip of a thing like you?"

"I could get used to this treatment," Scarlett told Randy.

The corners of Randy's mouth tipped upward at her, then he asked Preston, "So, are you going to be able to help me bring my semi home tomorrow?"

"Sure." He nodded.

"Great. We'll have to hurry. I have to pick up the truck and get my haul before they close at two. And I want to take Scarlett to the store to stock up on groceries."

Marie joined them, relinquishing a snoozing Hank to Scarlett's arms. She volunteered, "I'll take Scarlett shopping. I love to shop. I don't care what kind."

Randy glanced at Scarlett to see if she objected. She didn't seem to, so he nodded. "Thanks. That would help a lot."

A short while later, Randy and Scarlett walked back to the apartment and she said, "I like your friends."

Randy nodded. "They're good people."

"They seem like your family."

"As much of a family as I have."

Scarlett looked up at Randy's profile in the muted winter moonlight. He was so secure about himself. Nothing seemed to sour his good nature. He wasn't bitter or scared and he didn't hold a grudge against the parents he knew nothing about or the people who never adopted him. He accepted life as it was and enjoyed it. Scarlett wanted to be just like him.

When they entered the warmth of the apartment, Scarlett placed Hannah in her drawer and dropped onto the couch, exhausted. Randy glanced at his watch. Nine o'clock. He figured Scarlett'd be asleep within a half hour so he reached for the remote control and sat down. "I wonder what's on TV."

He'd go back to the bar as soon as the ladies were asleep.

At nine-thirty, Scarlett took Hannah into the bedroom to feed her.

Well, he couldn't just get up and leave the apartment right now. That would be rude. So, he waited.

Awhile later, Scarlett, dressed in a sweatsuit, emerged from the bedroom. "She's fast asleep."

Randy was engrossed in a rerun of *The Honeymooners*. I'll just watch this then go back to the bar, he told himself.

"Oh, I love this show!" Scarlett curled up on the couch to watch.

"Me, too."

"They don't make comedy like they used to." Scarlett sighed.

"You're right," he agreed, "They don't make anything like they used to. Take cartoons for instance."

Scarlett gave him a puzzled look. "Cartoons?"

"Yup. They used to be real works of art and entertainment."

"You watch cartoons?"

He nodded. "Every chance I get. I guess it's the artist in me."

"I saw the art books. Do you draw or paint?"

"Both, but neither very well. That's why I'm a trucker and not an artist."

"I'd love to see some of your work."

Few people knew of his hobby and the ones who did, with the exception of Preston and Marie, never asked to see his work. It had always been a private thing for him.

"Sure," he heard himself saying, "I'll show you sometime."

A particularly funny segment of the show caught their attention and eliminated conversation.

Randy turned off the television at eleven o'clock. He wouldn't go back to the bar. Scarlett was asleep and he was ready to get some rest himself.

I'm getting old.

Randy carried Scarlett to his bed and left her there in the darkness. It was the first time he could remember not joining a woman in his bed. But, tonight, Scarlett looked as innocent as Hank.

SIX

Scarlett gave Hannah an apprehensive look as Marie pushed down the gas pedal of her station wagon and they rocketed from the parking lot. The baby seemed content, but Scarlett didn't like her head being pressed against the seat by the force of the speeding vehicle.

"Preston thinks I'm a speed demon," Marie called over the roar of the engine, "He never rides with me."

Scarlett agreed with Preston. Southern people were infamous for moving at a slower pace than any other group in the country, but Marie could hold her own against any big-city traffic Scarlett had ever seen.

"Randy rides with me, though," Marie added with a smile.

Scarlett asked, "How long have you known Randy? You all seem to get along so well."

Marie's smile turned melancholy. "Randy's like the son we never had. He came here from Texas a little over four years ago. We had advertised the apartment and since it was so reasonable, he rented it right away. He was saving money for that truck even back then."

He'd saved that long for the truck and Scarlett managed to ruin its interior in less than a day? She felt like a criminal.

Scarlett sighed. "He felt I distracted him and caused him to lose control of the truck. I admit to ruining the seats. He must hate me."

Marie tilted her head and looked at Scarlett for a few moments. Scarlett wished she'd put her eyes back on the curving road. Aside from being uncomfortable with the expression in the older woman's eyes, there were also some *big* trees to sideswipe.

"I'll be honest with you," Marie finally said. "Randy was very angry about his truck. He's worked very hard for everything he's gotten in life, which is mainly that truck. He's never asked a soul for help and had a hard time accepting it when it was offered to him. But Randy's not the type to hold a grudge or hate anybody. He's a good man, Scarlett."

She was trying to tell Scarlett something. She didn't have to point out Randy was a good man. Scarlett knew that from firsthand experience. She also knew the roots of this woman's maternal feelings for Randy ran deep.

That incident with the table last night was Marie's way of discouraging all the female vultures from hovering over Randy. Wouldn't she be surprised to learn just how harmless they were in comparison to Scarlett?

Randy deserved a good woman. Everyone knew that even if he didn't, but Scarlett was not that woman. Relationships were hard enough if begun with a clean slate, but doomed if started with the problems she'd contribute.

Sadness and regret stabbed at Scarlett's heart and she stared out the window. In a different place and time—if she'd met Randy before Jonas—things might have been very different. As things were now, she not only had outside influences dictating her life, but she couldn't quite bring herself to trust any man—even Randy—after the men she'd known.

Marie pulled into the Dominion Grocery, turned off the car, and helped Scarlett with Hannah. The store was a flurry of activity with what seemed like the entire female population of Dominion. Marie explained that they congregated at the grocery store every Saturday morning for the social interaction as much as stocking up on provisions.

Marie selected a cart with the least wobbly wheels and they positioned Hannah in the top basket. As they walked along the aisles selecting various pieces of produce, cans of this and boxes of that, Scarlett began to feel paranoid. She'd been conditioned to watch her back and suspect everyone, but this was ridiculous. The women whose eyes she felt upon her were housewives. Some had never been farther from home than Wilmington. They married their high school sweethearts, had babies, and lived a quiet happy life. They wouldn't know how to be spies for Jonas if he offered them enough money to pay off the mortgage on the farm.

Scarlett supposed they were just curious.

Marie caught her anxiously glancing around every so often and patted her hand. "Don't worry too much about them. They're mostly just curious and they can't help but feel a little threatened."

"Threatened?" Scarlett's eyes widened.

Marie tilted her head, her eyes sparkling. "Well, you are a pretty little thing and you're a single woman."

Scarlett ran a caressing finger along Hannah's soft cheek. "A single woman with a baby."

As if she'd read Scarlett's earlier thoughts, Marie said, "Most of them married right after high school. They've never known a single woman with a baby who moved in with a single man."

Heat seared Scarlett's skin and she bowed her head. Marie crooked a finger beneath her chin and forced her to look up. "Scarlett, don't hang your head. Don't you ever hang your head or be ashamed. You have a beautiful daughter and you are doing the best you can for her. The circumstances surrounding her birth don't really matter, do they? What matters most is what *you* think. If you don't like something, then change it. Hanging your head's not the answer.''

"But I don't know what the answer is," Scarlett admitted.

Marie chuckled. "Few people ever do know the answers, my dear. You do the best you can." When Scarlett still didn't seem convinced, she added, "You aren't nearly as bad as you think you are. Maybe you ought to start looking at yourself though the eyes of those who care about you."

Scarlett blinked. "Who?"

"Well, Preston and me for starters . . . And, of course, Randy."

"Randy?" Scarlett blurted. She pushed the cart forward and pretended to read the back of a cereal box. "He's just a good Samaritan."

"He's a red-blooded American male."

"With an extremely active love life, which I don't want to ruin."

"Oh, go ahead and ruin it! He'll be thirty in three weeks. He needs to slow down. If he can't see that, then maybe it should be forced upon him."

Scarlett smiled, dropping the cereal into the cart. "But he doesn't *want* to slow down."

"Oh, pooh! What a man wants and what he thinks he wants are two different things, my dear."

"Well, I suppose he wouldn't have asked me to move in if he thought it would be a stumbling block to his social activities."

Marie's brow raised. "Or maybe that was his intention."

Scarlett eyed the tall woman for a moment. Had she decided Randy and his roomie were meant for each other? No.

"I'd think they'd be more jealous of Dixie than me," Scarlett said, more to herself than to Marie.

"Dixie?" Marie exclaimed. "Why would they be jealous of her?"

"Well, she and Randy seem very . . . close."

"They're friends. That's all."

Scarlett said nothing for a moment, wondering how Marie could be so sure. "Marie, what do you know about Dixie?"

Marie shrugged, tossing a box of Tuna Helper into the cart and moving down the aisle. Scarlett grimaced at the thought of tuna and returned the box to the shelf when Marie wasn't looking.

"What do you want to know?" Marie asked when Scarlett caught up with her.

"Have you ever met her? What's she like?"

"I used to wonder if she was real until she relayed a message to us from Randy when he was on the road. We've talked to her on the CB a lot since then, but we've never met her. She's nice. She's got three young kids of her own and custody of her teenage sister. I get the feeling she's a widow, but I'm not sure. Judging from the things she's done and what she talks about, I'd guess she's in her mid-thirties." Marie eyed Scarlett. "Have I covered it all?"

Scarlett wasn't sure.

The older woman patted her hand. "Dixie's like a big sister to him. They're friends and that's all. She's not a threat to *anyone*."

Scarlett sighed. Marie was giving her the "green" light to pursue Randy.

Dixie was no threat. She and Randy were just friends. Scarlett tamped down the pleasure that knowledge gave her. She knew Randy had a lot of women in his life, but she saw Dixie as the only serious one. Now she knew that was not true.

Yet, Scarlett had no right to find the news wonderful. Even if she wanted to become a part of Randy's life, it was out of the question. No matter what anyone else thought, there was no future for them.

For all she knew, *she* might not have a future at all.

*   *   *

"Mind telling me why we stopped here?" Preston asked as he leaned across the hood of the pickup and waited for Randy to climb out of the semi.

"I forgot to tell Scarlett to buy something."

Preston gave Randy a suspicious glance, then straightened and pulled out a pack of cigarettes to have a smoke. "Yeah, well, tell my bride to come out and keep me company, will you?"

"I won't be that long."

Preston nodded. "Sure you won't. Don't forget we have to pick up the load. They close in an hour."

Randy waved a hand as he entered the Dominion Grocery. He found Scarlett and Marie in the frozen-foods section, laughing like two teenagers.

Scarlett looked up in surprise. "Randy!"

"I stopped by because I forgot to tell you I needed some disposable razors for the trip." He really didn't and he didn't know why he stopped. He just did and he needed an excuse. Disposable razors were as good an excuse as any.

Scarlett smiled, reached into the cart and held up a package.

"Oh," Randy said, shoving his hands into the front pockets of his new indigo jeans.

"I got them just in case," Scarlett said.

"Women do that kind of thing, you know," Marie interjected. "You should get yourself one."

Randy blushed. Scarlett lowered her eyes on the pretense of replacing the razors in the cart.

"We're almost finished," Marie told him. "Why don't you help her, Randy? Just in case you forgot something else. Is Preston outside?"

Randy nodded.

He never thought buying groceries could be so awkward, but there was something almost intimate about deciding between chopped broccoli or florets.

As they passed the stand of paperback books at the end of the frozen foods aisle, Randy walked over to read the titles. Scarlett waited at the cart with Hannah and watched him grab a thick book.

"An instruction book." He grinned and showed her the title.

Scarlett laughed softly when she read it. *Bringing Up Baby, The Answers to New Parents' Questions*.

They shared a laugh, which came to an abrupt end when a sound as loud as a gun shot blasted behind them. Randy ducked and placed himself between the sound and Scarlett, who was leaning across her baby. Slowly they turned to discover a young woman dressed in a blue and khaki Dominion Grocery uniform standing in the frozen food aisle. Her hands rested upon her curved hips and anger made her lovely jaw appear plaster-hard. Between her spread feet lay the splinters of a wooden crate and scattered boxes of frozen fish sticks.

"Hello, Randy," the girl hissed.

"Hey, Stephanie," Randy said with apprehension.

Scarlett couldn't blame him. Stephanie's brown eyes gleamed with loathing. Her ample chest heaved with irritation. She wasn't the kind of woman to burst into tears from a love gone awry. She was the kind of woman to scoop up as many containers of frozen fish as she could hold in one arm and hurl them like a seasoned pitcher with the other.

Stephanie's eyes narrowed at Scarlett then zeroed-in on Randy like an armed missile. Stephanie heaved. She seethed. She clenched her fists into balls at her sides then reminded Randy in a high-pitched shriek, "You were supposed to call me, you pond scum!"

"Well—"

"I suppose you were too busy, huh?" Stephanie glanced at Scarlett and Hank again, but focused on Randy once more.

"Well—"

"To think that *I*, Stephanie Webster, actually waited by the phone for your call!"

"Hey, Stephanie, I'm really sorry. I just forgot—"

"You forgot?" Stephanie shouted back at him.

Scarlett groaned and shook her head. Randy really *should* slow down his love life. It was getting dangerous!

Stephanie became calm so fast it was spooky. She raised a hand. "No . . . no. Actually, I'm glad I found out you're the dirt on the belly of a worm before I really got involved. Then I'd be *really* angry."

"This isn't really angry?" Scarlett asked out of the corner of her mouth.

"We're leaving now, Steph," Randy called, motioning for Scarlett to duck around the shelves holding canned peas.

"Good! I don't ever want to see you again!"

Randy followed Scarlett as they hurried toward the check-out counter. He glanced over his shoulder to make sure Stephanie wasn't following with a jagged piece of wood aimed at his back.

"Are all your girlfriends like her?"

Scarlett's question brought Randy's head around to her direction. "She's not my girlfriend."

"Well, technically, now she's your ex-girlfriend—"

"She's not *any* form of girlfriend!"

Scarlett frowned. "She sure acts like your girlfriend."

"She's not," Randy assured her.

Something in his eyes warned her not to pursue this . . . or maybe begged was a better word. It felt as if he was trying to send her a message via mental telepathy, but she couldn't quite grasp all the words. She decided to let the subject die and moved behind the last woman in the check-out line.

Outside, Marie joined Preston, a smile on her full lips.

"Is it as bad as I think it is?" Preston asked.

"Oh, it's much worse."

Preston's brow lifted. "Not?"

"Love," Marie said.

"*Our* Randy?"

Marie's head bobbed up and down. "And Scarlett, too. Only they're both as blind as newborn pups."

"Lord have mercy! All hell's going to break loose when all these little local gals find out they worked so hard and an outsider snared Randy!"

Marie chuckled. "I seem to recall another group of unhappy girls a few years back."

Preston agreed, "You really upset a lot of beautiful young women when you caught me."

"There were a *few* unhappy girls, not a *lot*. Don't flatter yourself so much, my dear."

Preston smiled, then shot her a questioning glance. "Are you sure this girl's right for Randy? I mean, it's obvious she's running away from something. She's scared. What if there's some deep, dark secret she's hiding?"

"I don't know. I just have this feeling in my bones that she's the one for Randy."

"Well, you had a feeling in your bones about me and look how good we turned out."

"Yes, I always trust my feelings even if everyone tells me I'm wrong."

Preston flashed her a concerned look. "Everyone told you I was wrong for you?"

Marie gave him a shrug for an answer.

"You never told me that. Why didn't you tell me that? I want to know who said it and what they said."

Marie smiled and slipped her arms around his waist. "Shut up and give me a kiss."

Around noon on Sunday, Scarlett accompanied Randy to the parking lot to say good-bye. He stowed his duffel bag in the small sleeper behind the seats, then jumped out to kick the tires and double check the trailer hitches.

Scarlett watched in silence, her arms crossed to protect

herself against the cold even though she wore warm clothes.

"Well, that's it except for checking the gauges," Randy said as he walked toward her. "You ought to go inside."

She shrugged and looked at the rig. "You'd never know the truck sailed across a ditch, would you? The repair people did a good job."

Randy nodded in agreement. He hoped they didn't get another snowstorm. It was colder than a witch's heart today. Headed for Atlanta, he stood a good chance of bypassing a major blizzard, but he wasn't sure Dominion would be so lucky.

"Now, you have Preston and Marie's number if you need anything. They live a half mile up the road so they can be here quickly, although they're at the bar most of the time. I left the key to the pickup on the kitchen table just in case."

Her eyes widened in surprise. "You trust me with a vehicle?"

"Only in case of extreme emergency. It's an old vehicle, you'll note. And," he said, draping an arm over her shoulder so he could turn her toward the highway, "see that thing out there made of asphalt with lines on it? That's the road. You're supposed to keep the truck on that."

Scarlett looked up at him, faking amazement. "Really? I never knew that!"

They smiled at each other and Randy's eyes dropped to her full lips for a long time before he broke away and headed for the truck. He said over his shoulder, "I'll try to give you a call and don't expect me back before Tuesday."

Randy climbed into the cab, trying to concentrate on the gauges before him, instead of the blonde standing a few feet from the truck. He'd never had anyone stand there and watch him leave before. It sent a jolting current of something through him—something he attempted to shove aside by turning the truck's key. Even the semi's purr to life didn't cover up the pounding of his heart.

As he shifted into gear and pulled out of the parking lot, Randy tossed Scarlett a quick wave.

He imagined this was the scene married truckers played every time they went on a haul. Except they probably made love with their ladies and kissed them good-bye, instead of just thinking about it.

"Now, let me get this straight," Dixie said Tuesday afternoon when Randy finally established contact with her. "You went to the hospital, picked up Scarlett and her baby, and they're now living with you?"

"Yup."

"Don't that cramp your style?"

"Yup."

"Then why'd you do it?"

Randy shrugged, although Dixie couldn't see that over the CB. "Don't know."

"You don't know?" Dixie sighed. "Star, I'm beginning to wonder about you."

"I'm beginning to wonder about me, too," he mumbled.

"What was that?"

"Nothing."

"Yeah, right . . . Well, how's the baby?"

"I guess she's okay. I mean, I don't have any knowledge of babies so I have nothing to compare her to."

"Does she sleep?"

"Yup."

"Does she eat?"

"I guess so."

There was a long silence before Dixie told him in a controlled voice, "Your answers to my questions are starting to annoy me. What the hell does 'I guess so' mean? Is the child plump or emaciated? How hard is it to tell if she eats?!"

Randy knew Dixie well enough to know she was not as angry as she sounded.

"She feeds her in privacy."

"Why? Is she ashamed of the baby? Does she spit her milk at passersby?"

He also knew Dixie well enough to know she was going to thoroughly enjoy his next statement. "She does it for my benefit. She breast-feeds."

As Dixie's silence lengthened, Randy's face reddened. Her burst of laughter came as a relief.

"You really are a piece of work, Star! You can take a near-stranger to bed, but you can't watch a woman breast-feed! How can you be embarrassed by her breasts when you've seen her—"

"I was embarrassed by that, too, Dixie! Okay?" Randy shouted, realizing they were on the open air and he didn't know who might be listening. He sighed. "Damn, Dixie, this is so different."

"Different?"

"From my dealings with other women. I *have* taken them to bed, but . . ."

"But you've delivered Scarlett's child."

"Yeah," Randy almost groaned.

"And you've had to share things like the refrigerator and bathroom with her."

"Yeah."

"And you've *talked* to her."

"At this point that's all I can do," he mumbled then added quickly, "not that I want to do anything more with Scarlett than talk."

"Um–hm."

"Really . . . I kind of like talking to her."

"Uh–oh."

"Don't say that! The last time someone said that to me, I almost got killed and had to deliver a baby!"

"And caught Scarlett fever. Ten-four, good buddy!"

* * *

By the time Randy reached home, he'd worked himself up so much his nervous energy could power a submarine. The trip was easy, but it gave him too much time to think.

He thought about work. He needed something other than these short, sporadic hauls to keep him going. He needed a broker. Without one, an independent trucker couldn't survive. So far, not a single broker had returned his calls.

He couldn't admit defeat, especially since he had an infant under his roof he felt responsible for.

Which brought him to the second thing occupying his mind. He'd done a lot of thinking about what Dixie said since they talked.

Scarlett fever?

Like hell!

Not this single man. He liked to talk to Scarlett. He'd even admit he liked to fight with her. And for some ungodly reason his hormones reverted back to primitive adolescent stages most of the time they were together, but was that fever?

N–O.

He was free. Free to come and go as he pleased. Free to eat what he wanted when he wanted. He could walk around in his underwear and sing the "Star Spangled Banner" without having a woman nag him . . .

Well, he could when Scarlett moved out, anyway . . .

The sun had almost set, casting a pale pink light on Dominion when he parked the semi at the back of Preston's. Clouds, like scoops of blueberry ice cream, hung heavy in the sky. The air pinched his exposed cheeks and nose when he stepped from the truck.

Randy pulled up the fleece-lined collar of his denim jacket, grabbed his duffel bag, and secured the rig. He turned and stared at Preston's.

Music and laughter licked at his ears. The tangy aroma of peppered steaks searing on the grill tickled his nose and tempted his taste buds. The thoughts of settling back to unwind with an ice cold beer seemed mighty good right now.

Then he looked up at his apartment.

The window was filled with a warm glow. In all his years of being on the road and coming home, there'd never been a light on in the window. No one ever waited for his return.

Randy ambled toward the building and instead of taking the well-worn path to the bar, he climbed the stairs to his apartment.

At the door, Randy paused. The television was blaring and he thought he heard Hank crying. Just in case Scarlett was nursing—though he couldn't see how if Hank's mouth was open—he knocked.

The door flung open.

Randy stepped back.

Sounds from the TV blasted his eardrums. The sight before him blasted his eyes.

Scarlett stood in the doorway, her chest heaving, her teeth clenched. One hand gripped the door, the other pressed against the jamb. What Randy thought might have once been a ponytail crept down the back of her head in a lopsided path. Escaping strands fell about her face like frayed electrical wires. Dark crescents hung beneath her puffy, red-rimmed eyes.

She's been crying again. I passed up Preston's for this?

"Forget your key?" Scarlett asked in a tone as brittle as her features.

"Good lord, woman! What the *hell* happened to you?" Randy's eyes dropped to her feet and ran back up her shell-shot form.

"Motherhood." Scarlett tossed at him over her shoulder as she headed for the couch.

He followed her into the living room. "Correct me if I'm wrong, but weren't you a mother before I left?"

Scarlett's eyes narrowed.

He sighed then turned down the volume on the TV and dropped onto the recliner. "Want to talk about it?"

She pointed toward the bedroom. "Hear that? She hasn't stopped crying since Sunday. The *bar* called to complain about the noise."

Randy coughed to cover up his laugh.

"You laugh."

Randy tried to be sympathetic. "Is she sick?"

Scarlett shook her head. "She hasn't got a fever. She's not had a sick stomach. She's been eating like a pig."

"Well, why don't we take a look at her?"

"You take a look. I've looked at her from top to bottom."

Randy walked to the bedroom, opened the door and winced at the sound of Hank's wails.

"Hey!" Randy stomped to the bed and glared down into the drawer. "Stop that racket, little woman! You're driving your mom crazy!"

The baby stopped crying. No aftershocks. No stray tears. Just silence.

Randy stepped back in surprise.

"Hey!" Scarlett rounded the doorway, her face covered with worry. "I wanted her to stop crying. I didn't want you to execute her!"

She stared down at her daughter who lounged in her drawer as contented as a cream-fed kitten. Hannah's tiny mouth puckered and pursed. Her little hands balled into fists and extended as if she were an adolescent checking her nail polish. Gone were the furrows of discontent from her miniature brow.

Scarlett glared at Randy. "Okay. What was the drug?"

"What drug?"

"The drug you slipped my daughter!"

Randy's expression became smug. "No drug. You just have to know how to deal with infants."

Scarlett crossed her arms. "Spoken from the mouth of a professed child hater."

"You don't have to love them to know how to deal with them." He lifted the drawer. "You look as if you're sick of each other. I'll take her into the living room. You get some rest."

Scarlett didn't argue.

As Randy left the bedroom, he whispered to Hank, "You remember this, because when you can talk I want you to tell me what I did to shut you up."

Randy spent the next two days helping Preston at the bar. He told himself it was because he wanted to keep busy, but he knew it was because of what Dixie said. Just in case anyone else was getting the same impression of him, he wanted to prove he hadn't been domesticated yet.

So, even though he'd been away for a few days, he distanced himself from Scarlett—for appearances' sake.

Some of his old flames made the effort to rekindle the fire, but they didn't strike a spark. The girls he once found delicious now seemed dull.

He still needed a woman—the haul hadn't been very fruitful for him in that respect—but he also needed more than just a warm body beneath him.

His old buddies didn't seem the same either. The guys he once partied with now acted mighty immature. Only the three he played an occasional game of poker with were palatable.

Randy attributed these feelings to his thirtieth birthday coming up soon. It rearranged his standards.

On Thursday night, a local factory owner offered him work for Friday. Two of the man's three trucks were broken down and there were special deliveries in Raleigh and Fayetteville on top of the regular stops. It was only for one day, but it was work.

Shortly after seven on Friday night, Randy walked through the door to be blessed with a tidy apartment and the aroma of something spicy cooking.

Scarlett sat on the sofa, her hair pulled back in a neat

braid. She'd donned the same skirt and sweater she'd worn to Preston's last Saturday. It occurred to Randy there was only so much you could stuff into two shoulder bags. He'd buy both ladies of the house some new clothes if he ever made some money.

"Hi!" Scarlett stood up.

Randy shed his coat and Stetson, dropped them onto a chair by the table and looked about. "The place looks nice."

Scarlett beamed. "Thanks. It took me most of the day. I'd clean for ten minutes, then rest for twenty."

"You didn't have to do this."

Her eyes didn't blink for a long time. "Yes, I did." She walked to the stove. "I know I'm taking a chance on this since you're from the heart of Tex-Mex food, but I had a Mexican friend in California who taught me to cook some of her favorites."

Randy's head jerked up. California. Scarlett was from California? Did she offer this information freely or did she slip up?

"It's the only thing I can cook." She turned back and smiled, either not realizing what she said or not caring that she had. Did she trust him now?

"Smells great and I'm starved," Randy said, trying not to indicate something extraordinary had just occurred.

"Oh." She moved to the phone and picked up a note pad. "This man called for your today. He wanted you to call him back no matter what time you got in . . . a Mr. Killigrew."

"That's a broker!" Randy reached for the phone and dialed the number.

Scarlett walked to the stove. She spooned seasoned vegetables and deep-dish Mexican casserole onto two plates while Randy carried on a brief conversation with Mr. Killigrew.

Randy returned the phone to the cradle. He whirled about, barely giving Scarlett time to put the plates on the table before he lifted her by her waist. "He's short a driver for the next few weeks!"

He twirled about in a circle and Scarlett placed a hand on each of his shoulders for support.

Laughing, she asked, "This is good?"

His arms encircled her and he allowed her to slide down the length of his body until her breasts rested against his collarbone. She was gazing down at him. At this close range, he could see there was not another color in her eyes, but cool, lush green. Even her freckles couldn't mar her flawless skin. She was beautiful and she smelled of soap and flowers.

"Oh, yes," he said in a hoarse, husky voice. "This is very good."

His double entendre left her blushing, but she didn't resist his hold upon her. So, he held her for a long time before letting her stand on her own feet and dropping his arms to his side.

"The driver was going to take a haul to Texas. Mr. Killigrew knew I grew up in Texas so he decided to give me a chance. If this works out, he'll sign me on."

"That's wonderful, Randy!"

"I'll be gone for about seven days."

"Oh . . . When do you leave?"

"Tomorrow morning at six sharp. I have to pick up the load in Wilmington."

"Tomorrow morning? Get your butt in gear, Mister! We have laundry to do!"

By ten thirty, the laundry was done and Scarlett had packed more underwear than Randy thought he owned. He supposed those things really mattered to women—clean underwear and such.

Scarlett fed and bathed Hank. They ate the meal that would have been much tastier an hour and a half before, then spent ten minutes arguing over who would get the bed and who would get the sofa.

Randy gave in, closed the bedroom door behind him and fell into bed exhausted.

By eleven o'clock, all was quiet in Randy's world.

An hour later, Hank's banshee-like wails speared through the silence and threatened to dissolve Randy's teeth. He rolled onto his stomach and covered his head with a pillow.

When Randy could take no more, he peaked from under the pillow and stared bleary eyed at the clock radio's illuminated numbers.

Ten after two.

Patience snapped, tired, and remembering he had to rise and shine at five, Randy kicked off the covers. He pulled on his robe and stomped toward the door.

"Dammit, woman!" He bolted into the living room. "Can't you do something with that child?"

Scarlett turned on him, frazzled and seething. "If I knew what to do, dammit, don't you think I'd do it?"

Randy's eyes dropped to the baby. Her tiny fists were clenched defiantly. Her toothless mouth formed a large oh, filling her entire face with the exception of two squiggly marks taking the place of her eyes.

"A muzzle might work!"

"Have you got one?" Scarlett returned.

Randy looked at her. He wasn't serious about the muzzle, but she appeared to be. "Well, what's wrong with her?"

"Haven't got a clue."

"Gas?"

Scarlett rolled her eyes. "I've burped her, bounced her, and bribed her, and she won't quit crying."

"What did the instruction book say?"

"I'm burning that book, do you hear me? I could learn more about this child from a *Farmer's Almanac*!"

Randy grimaced when Hank hit a new high note. "Well, there must be something you can do. I need my rest."

As soon as he said it, Randy regretted those words. Scarlett, as weary and irritable as he was, didn't need his demands. Her expression evolved into a cross between *The Creature From Outer Space* and *Two Thousand Maniacs*.

"Do you think this is music to my ears, Bucko?" She stepped forward. He stepped back.

"Well, I—"

"Do you think that when I found out I was pregnant I begged God to give me a child whose cry would harden my spinal fluid?"

She moved toward him. He moved equal distance away.

"Well, I—"

"It's not easy being a mother, Randy! I can't tell a note's difference between her hungry cry and her wet-bottom cry." A sob caught in her throat.

Uh–oh. She's gonna cry.

He took one more defensive step and backed into the wall, causing the quartz clock above his shoulder to rock wildly. For a moment, they both watched the timepiece threaten to leap from the wall, then steady itself and come to rest cockeyed on the nail.

Scarlett's eyes focused on Randy. "I've had it with you thinking I'm a miracle worker. If you think it's so easy—here, you do it!"

With that, Scarlett deposited her daughter into Randy's unskilled hands.

SEVEN

Randy accepted the child with arms as stiff as oak boughs. But what else could he do? Scarlett had stepped away and he wasn't about to play a game of hot potato with an infant.

As soon as Hank's little body fit into Randy's hands, her mouth clamped shut and her eyes popped open.

The change so surprised Randy he wished he *had* tossed Hank back to her mother. Something overcame him when the baby ceased crying at mere contact with him. Something strange and wonderful and scary all at the same time.

If a new father felt like this, he supposed parenthood was worth it.

Of course, Randy was the first to hold Hank. He'd been the one to clean out her mouth and hand her to her mom, but he'd never experienced this feeling. But then a lot was happening the night Hank entered the world and he was a bit dazed. Still, he thought he might recall something like this no matter what kind of trance he was in.

It was as if someone had injected warm cognac into his veins.

The baby liked him. There was no denying that *he* was

116

the reason she stopped crying. *His* touch. *His* voice. This was some ego booster.

Randy traced her fat little cheek with his finger and she seized it with her miniscule hand. The baby grip electrified his senses. His throat constricted and, as he gazed down into the wide blue eyes fixed upon him, his heart pounded in his chest.

She *was* rather pretty now that he studied her. The pug nose, the round cheeks, the prominent drool-streaked chin all had a certain appeal. She smelled of baby powder and shampoo and she made contented grunts and clucks that were uniquely her own.

Randy was smitten. When someone as small and innocent as Hank found him irresistible, he couldn't help but reciprocate. If she saw something worth loving in him, he must not be too bad.

Then Randy recalled this was not his baby and this was not his woman standing a few feet away. They belonged to Jonas, or at least his memory, and Randy had no stake on them. They weren't permanent fixtures in his life and he'd be a fool if he got attached to this kid only to have her taken from him. It was just a matter of time before Scarlett decided to leave. He knew it and she knew it.

It was just as well, he decided, because he was not the type to settle down, nor was Scarlett ready for a relationship.

When Hank stopped crying, Scarlett had been prepared to fly off the handle. She was Hannah's mother and should supply her baby's every need. Yet, Randy had just accomplished in seconds what Scarlett had worked toward for hours. But when she looked at Randy's face, something had changed.

Something about him had softened . . . or maybe melted. His features had never been harsh before, but now they were mellow and tender.

So much became clear to Scarlett now. Hannah's first

tantrum occurred when Randy was out of town. This one was on the eve of his leaving. Either the child sensed he was going on the road again or she just needed his attention. After all, he hadn't touched her since that first night.

One word, one touch from Randy soothed the baby into a state of euphoria. She'd bonded to him. Trusted him. Loved him. Maybe even thought of him as her father, if babies thought in those terms.

Scarlett would be hard pressed to find a better man than Randy for her baby's father. Maybe he wasn't wealthy with money, but he possessed the attributes that really mattered. He could love someone. He was kind and generous and he'd already given Hannah the kind of home Scarlett always wished for herself.

No, there weren't expensive paintings on the walls or fancy china on the table; there was not a maid or a butler ready to answer every whim of a spoiled adult.

This was a safe and stable environment to raise a child. This was a homey atmosphere. This was a man with scruples and honor who could laugh and enjoy life. A man who could kiss a bruised knee and make it better. A man who could mend a bruised heart.

Scarlett almost laughed at the irony of this situation. She'd found a man she could respect and possibly one day come to love, a man Hannah had chosen for her father, and to keep him safe she had to leave him.

Jonas would one day catch up with her; his pride would never allow him to just give up. And his bruised, maniacal ego would not allow her to escape retribution for running from him.

The stakes had become too high for her to take Jonas lightly—not that she ever had. He'd already hurt people because of her. When she'd called some of those who'd helped her along the way, they'd told her how a man named Jonas asked about her. When they gave him no information, crops mysteriously burned up in the fields, farm animals died from eating poison, and store inventories just disappeared.

Jonas was a sick man. The thin thread dangling him over the edge of insanity could have already snapped. She shuddered to think what Jonas might do to Randy, who had nothing in this world but that truck . . . and his life.

Fear and regret marred the beautiful picture before her.

She could at least accept the consequences of her own mistakes, but she'd drawn innocent people into the avalanche of her bad choices. She jeopardized her baby's happiness and could possibly ruin the life of a man who'd become very important to her.

Her only defense was to run and she'd do just that when she was able.

Randy raised his eyes. His Adam's apple bobbed up and down as he swallowed over and over. When he spoke, his voice was almost as raspy as hers. "Well, she's quiet. Here."

Scarlett took the baby and waited to see if there'd be another outburst. There wasn't. By the time Scarlett lay Hannah in the drawer, she was fast asleep.

Randy stood near the bedroom door and watched Scarlett administer the motherly touch to her child. This mother-child bond amazed him. Scarlett had carried the baby for nine months, gone through hours of agony just to give Hank life, and been robbed of sleep thanks to the kid's marathon tantrums . . . Yet, look at her. She loved the child. She was tender with her.

He found himself wondering what it took for a mother to quit loving a child as small as Hank. More specifically, what had he done when he was a newborn to make his mother leave him in an orphanage?

"Randy, what's wrong?" Scarlett asked, her voice tainted with alarm as she turned to look at him.

Randy's eyes darted upward as he realized he was leaning against the wall and staring at the floor. He slipped his hands into the pockets of his robe and shrugged. "Nothing."

She crossed the room to touch his arm. "You looked as though you'd seen a ghost. Something's wrong."

He pasted a smile on his face and gazed deeply into her eyes. "I was just thinking that you'd better lock Hank in her room at the first signs of puberty, if she reacts that way to a guy like me."

Scarlett looked up at him and in her most sincere voice, she said, "I was just thinking that maybe she's a better judge of character than either you *or* me."

Their eyes held onto each other for a long time. It was as if he'd reached out and touched her face. The electricity and warmth that passed through them was as real as any caress. When he came to his senses and reminded himself for a lot of reasons he'd better turn away, he did just that. "Well, I think I'll go back to bed."

The road didn't hold the excitement for him that Randy once knew. There were long stretches of time to think that left him wound like a spring. Even a drink at the end of the day didn't help him unwind.

Randy refused to delve into his feelings too deeply, though. He was afraid of what he'd find. He didn't want to know what he felt for anyone. One thing the orphanage taught him was to keep things light and accept relationships as if they were cream floating on the top of a pail of milk. Don't skim too much off the surface and you'll always have the best.

Even being in Texas again didn't make an impression upon him. Instead of the fond memories he'd made after leaving the home, he remembered his days as an unwanted child.

Randy realized he was feeling sorry for himself and that was unlike him. So, on his one night's layover in Houston he decided to visit one of his old hangouts—a saloon called Spurs.

None of the old crowd was there, although he didn't expect them to be. It'd been nearly five years since he left Houston. The smells of smoke and beer and Spurs' famous barbecued ribs embraced him like a long lost friend, even if he couldn't find familiar human company.

He claimed a spot at the bar to lean against, ordered a beer, and turned to watch the dance floor. It'd been awhile since he'd seen the Texas Two-Step performed by real Texans and he enjoyed their expertise.

"You haven't been here before."

Randy turned toward the feminine voice and coughed at the sight before him. She was a brilliant redhead, almost as tall as he was. She wore skintight jeans over shapely hips and legs that didn't seem to stop. Her pink sweater hung off one tanned shoulder and drew attention to her ample bosom.

Randy ran an appraising eye over her because a woman like her expected it. When he found her face again, she smiled. She had a pretty smile and a pretty face. Her features were delicate and smooth, but her blue eyes were cold. There wasn't any pain or experience in them. Oh, she had the kind of experience she advertised by her clothing, he was sure. But she didn't have struggling and loss and well-earned happiness showing in the depths of her baby blues.

Randy knew the type. She was probably some oil magnate's spoiled brat out looking for someone to bring home and shock the old man.

"No. I don't get into town much." He took a chug from his beer. "I'm a trucker."

Her eyes sparkled like expensive sapphires. "A trucker."

Pay dirt. Randy knew she thought he'd be just the right pawn to send her father's blood pressure soaring to a stroke-threatening level.

She offered him her hand. "I'm Lacey Provost."

"Randy Taylor."

"Would you like to dance? Your beer will be fine right

here.'' She called over the bar, "Hey, Rafe! Take care of our beers, okay?''

A lanky man at the taps nodded and Randy found himself on the dance floor. He took Lacey into his arms, pulling her generous curves toward him as close as the Two-Step called for.

It'd been a long time since he'd done this. The folks in Dominion liked to Shag. The native Texas dance came back to him like riding a bicycle. He and Lacey danced for three consecutive songs, then made their way back to the bar where Rafe handed them cold replacements for their now-warm beers.

"You dance very well," Lacey commented, pushing her mane of hair from her face, "but your conversational skills don't match.''

Randy blinked at her. He hadn't said one word the whole time they danced, now that he thought about it. That wasn't like him. No, that wasn't like him at all. But then, he'd been doing a lot of things he wasn't used to lately.

"I guess I have a lot on my mind.'' He glanced about the bar.

"I see . . . Well, you just stick with me for the evening and I'll get whoever she is off your mind.'' Lacey curled a hand around his bicep and fit her body against his side.

His head jerked back in her direction just in time to receive her hot and hungry kiss.

Scarlett found herself glancing at the phone for the hundredth time on Tuesday night. Randy said he'd call, but he'd been gone three days and she'd heard nothing from him.

Not that she really expected him to call. He was under no obligation to her and he *was* on his old turf. He had probably looked up old friends and was having a great time—which he deserved, she reminded herself.

Scarlett looked at the clock. Eleven-thirty. She had a

hard time remembering which time zone Texas was in. Was it ten-thirty or nine-thirty there?

A thought occurred to Scarlett and she frowned. He might be in the arms of a beautiful woman. Randy was a red-blooded American male and as far as she knew, he'd not been with a woman in Dominion since she had moved in. She realized that her living at his apartment put a damper on his love life, but he hadn't even attempted to form a liaison.

So, he must have a woman on the road. A person didn't get a reputation like Randy's by abstaining. Besides that, a healthy young man like Randy wouldn't go without sex for over two weeks.

Would he?

Scarlett gazed down at Hannah. "Come on, tell me. You know him better than I do."

Hannah's eyes squinted and Scarlett sighed. "I know. You think your mother's a dingbat just like he does." Scarlett lifted Hannah and walked toward the window to stare out at the darkness concealing Dominion.

"Why do I care what Randy's doing, you're probably asking. After all, I plan to leave in a few weeks anyway. It's just that . . . Well, kiddo, I guess I'm thinking about what might have been. What life would have been like if I'd met Randy before I met Jonas."

Scarlett stared down at the cars surrounding Preston's and let out another sigh. Her eyes diverted back to Hannah, who yawned.

Scarlett laughed. "Boring stuff? Okay, are you trying to tell me all men are alike and it just takes longer for some to show their true colors than others?" She arched a blond brow. "Or are you trying to tell me Randy's different? What *is* on your mind?"

No matter what Hannah said, all men *were* alike. At least they were in Scarlett's life. Memories tumbled across her mind like dry sagebrush. She recalled the years spent with her father in that two-room shack in the Nevada desert and later in the seedy motel rooms in Las Vegas. Good old dad never ceased to remind her she owed him simply because he was her parent. He even tried to make her quit school and join him in the casinos.

Scarlett had seen what went on in there and it held no appeal for her. Perhaps she had only been exposed to the harsher side of gambling, but she refused to become a part of it. She'd stood her ground and continued school, hoping to make something of herself one day.

Yet, in fairness, Scarlett admitted marrying Jonas hadn't been entirely to clear her father's gambling debts. She saw it as a ticket to a better life, but any way you looked at it, she'd sold herself. So what did that make her? All the showers and denials in the world couldn't erase the dirt of that one hard, cold fact.

Jonas took great pleasure in adding to her guilt and shame. However, he didn't get the results he probably expected. Instead of pulling her toward him, he pushed her away and killed all the love she thought she had for him. She'd learned some hard lessons about believing in men—she couldn't. But here was Randy tempting her with his gentle ways and sweet smile. She was afraid she'd make a fool of herself again. She couldn't chance it.

She sighed and told Hannah, "Your mom makes bad choices. The only safe thing for us is to keep it just you and me, kid."

The phone's high-pitched ring dissolved Scarlett's newfound strength. She snatched the receiver from its cradle. "H-Hello?"

"Scarlett? Did I wake you? What time is it there?" Randy said, his voice husky with fatigue.

Randy looked about his motel room for his watch. He caught sight of himself in the mirror and yanked the sheet from the bed to wipe the pink lipstick off his cheek and lips, then he stuffed his shirt back into his pants and ran his fingers through his tangled hair.

"You didn't wake me. I was just feeding Hannah."

"How is she?"

Scarlett smiled, her mood becoming lighter as the subject centered around her child. "Great. Marie and I took her for her first checkup today. She's a bit small, but healthy as a horse."

Randy sat down on the bed and smiled. "That's good. Has she had any more tantrums?"

"No. I got smart. I didn't wash your robe and I laid it in her drawer. She sleeps like a baby!"

Randy laughed. "I can't believe that kid."

"Well, Randy, you *are* the only man she's ever come in contact with."

Randy heaved a big sigh and changed the subject. "So what have you been doing?"

"I must be getting better. I'm getting bored. I talked to Preston about working at the bar a few hours a day."

"Are you sure you're up to it?"

"He's going to let me run the cash register a few hours a night starting next week. That's three weeks since I gave birth. I think I'll be okay. I can always make change sitting down. I might have to supplement the breast-feeding with bottles."

Silence thickened the air and Scarlett's heartbeat quickened. *Say something. I need to hear your voice.*

When he said nothing, Scarlett finally asked, "So, how was your trip? Anything exciting happen?"

Randy's eyes dropped to the lipstick stains on the sheet and the empty beer bottles on the table. "No, nothing exciting. I guess I'd better go. I'll be home Friday. You take care."

"Okay. Good night, Randy."

"Good night, Scarlett."

Scarlett stared at the phone for a long time. He'd been with a woman . . .

. . . He'd been without a woman too long. Randy hung up and stared at the phone a long time before he stretched out on the bed, hands clasped behind his back, and stared at the ceiling.

The image of the disgruntled, unsatisfied redhead who stomped from his motel room came to mind. He'd brought Lacey back here with every intention of finally alleviating his sexual frustration, but when the crucial moment came, he chickened out. He wasn't prepared and he was not going to do anything with her without protection. She assured him she was on the pill, but pregnancy was only one of his worries.

But now that he was alone, he also realized that he didn't want to jump into bed with just anyone. He wasn't in the market anymore for just "a good lay" and it would take more than a beautiful body to satisfy the tension mounting in his body right now.

Confused and uptight, Randy stripped and went to the bathroom. Maybe a nice hot shower would loosen up his knotted muscles. It occurred to him as he was drying himself off that he'd had a half-naked gorgeous female literally throw herself upon him. Not only had he asked her to leave, but he hadn't needed a cold shower to erase the effects of her from his body.

Randy reached Dominion before sunrise on Friday morning, let himself into his quiet apartment, and found Hank in her drawer on the kitchen table.

He smiled down at the sleeping baby, noting how much she'd changed in a week. She'd filled out and was not nearly so blotchy. Her hair was longer and curled up at the ends now.

Randy felt grubby and wanted to take a shower. He didn't think the water running would disturb Scarlett since she was in the bedroom with the door closed, but he couldn't use his robe since it was a part of Hank's crib now.

He walked into the bathroom, turned on the water,

stripped, then took a towel from the linen closet and hung it on the hook behind the door.

When the water was the right temperature, Randy stepped inside, placed a hand on either side of the shower head, and allowed the water to pound away the grime of the trip.

About five minutes later he thought he heard something. *Was that Hank?*

He shut off the water and listened.

Yup. That was Hank.

Randy got out of the shower and grabbed the towel as he opened the bathroom door. It was early yet. He'd just quiet Hank and let Scarlett sleep a bit longer.

Too late.

Scarlett was already at the table. As Randy stepped from the bathroom, she swung around and they both froze. Randy stopped in the middle of wrapping the towel about his hips and Scarlett halted her turn to give him the best view of her breast-feeding Hank.

Scarlett's eyes followed a stream of water dripping from a tendril of hair against his right shoulder. She followed the water as it sluiced over his collar bone and picked the path of least resistance through the saturated sable pelt covering his chest. She boldly watched it roll across the peaks and valleys of his stomach as it successfully detoured the pitfall of getting lost in his navel, then took an angled trek toward his left side. Her eyes never strayed when the water came to a halt, nestling in the curls of hair at the groove between thigh and groin.

Then her eyes left the drop of water and gazed at the hub of his lower body.

Randy's eyes wasted no time centralizing on *her* exposed breast. In fact, they made a beeline to the soft mound. He followed the gentle swell of cleavage, paused to contemplate a mole in the dip between her breasts—sexy—and moved on to the point that interested Hank the most. The baby's nose was pressed against the strawberry-colored aureole. She tugged the nipple into her mouth with a vengeance.

Randy envied the child her position.

Scarlett was like a decadent dessert and Randy's mouth was watering. The rest of his body was beginning to react in a much more grownup male way.

His eyes lifted to find her blatantly staring at his growing arousal, that Mona Lisa smile making an appearance again. He tugged the towel about his hips.

She looked at him with disappointed eyes.

"You were staring," he said.

"So were you," she pointed out.

"*I've* never seen a woman nursing a baby before." His look challenged her to say she'd never seen a naked man since the proof that she had was lying in her arms.

Well, Scarlett couldn't say she'd never seen a naked man. But she could say she'd never seen one like Randy.

There'd been two men in her life. The first was a boy in her twelfth grade French class. They'd plunged past the point of heavy petting in the back seat of his car on prom night. It'd been an embarrassing, blundering mistake that she regretted. Her humiliation was heightened by the fact that the space was too cramped for any enjoyment and she caught only glimpses of the boy's anatomy in the pale moonlight.

The other man was Jonas. She'd always thought he was the most well-built man she'd ever seen. Thousands of dollars of exercise equipment, his own personal trainer, and two weeks a year at the most expensive spas around the world kept him in top physical condition.

Yes, she thought he looked mighty fine until a few moments ago when she saw Randy's body. She'd once thought of him as skinny and reevaluated him to lean. Now that she'd seen him naked, she knew both descriptions were wrong.

Randy had no fat on him. Underneath the smooth, richly toned skin were well-defined muscles and sinew, sculpted and molded for the sole purpose of catching a woman's breath.

His legs weren't the match sticks so many men possessed. Like his arms, they were strong, powerful, muscular. His chest seemed much more massive than when hidden beneath a shirt.

A vee-shaped patch of fur swept across his chest and dove downward until it united with the curls cradling his manhood. Her suspicions were now confirmed—Randy was a very well-formed, far-from-lanky, fully-grown *man*.

Blushing, Scarlett smiled at the baby nursing at her breast. "See. It's not as disgusting as you thought, is it?"

"I never thought it was disgusting, Scarlett," Randy assured her. "I just thought it was a private thing I shouldn't share."

"Randy, you shared her birth," Scarlett said simply, as if that were reason for anything.

All the doubts and uncertainties faded. He'd toyed with the idea, but now he *knew* he wanted to make love with this woman. He wanted to hold Scarlett and kiss her from head to toe. He wanted to caress her and taste her. He wanted to feel her beneath him and on top of him.

He knew no substitute would suffice the growing need inside him. That was why he'd sent Lacey away. When it was straight golden locks he wanted to twist around his fingers, red waves wouldn't do. A slow Texas drawl just didn't make it when he wanted to hear that raspy, west coast accent cry out his name. He knew he could turn out the lights and close his eyes and no other woman could replace Scarlett.

Maybe he *did* have Scarlett fever. Lust was a kind of fever.

So, because no one else would do and he wasn't the kind to take just anyone for the sake of release—he liked to think he had control over himself—he'd wait until Scarlett was physically capable of making love with him.

Hell, it would probably take him that long to warm her up to the idea.

But he had to know one thing.

"Scarlett." He stared deep into her eyes. "Are you married?"

Scarlett tensed at his question. Not so much from the question itself—it was perfectly normal to want to know if the person you lived with was married—but from the questions that might follow.

She took a deep breath and then took a chance. She answered him honestly. "No, Randy, I'm not married."

He searched her face for the truth, then he looked down at the floor. For the first time, he saw the pool of water gathering beneath his feet. "I guess I'd better dry off before I flood the place."

Randy was home for one day. Mr. Killigrew called him with another emergency that afternoon and he was on the road again bright and early the next day. The difference was this time he had a copy of a signed contract in his glove compartment. Randy now had a broker who could line up jobs for him.

He spent most of the next few weeks on the road, coming into Dominion for a day here, two days there. That time was spent catching up on his sleep, working on his truck, and helping Scarlett with the heavy housework. He also spent a lot of time with Hank and found he really liked the kid. She didn't do a whole lot, but she had potential.

Most of Randy and Scarlett's "quality time" was spent over the phone hundreds of miles apart. He'd begun to think of her as a second Dixie.

Randy was used to being on the road, but he wasn't used to such long hauls. Yet, the money was good and he had a long weekend scheduled off at the end of the month, as well a week or so the first of February. He was looking forward to being home and relaxing.

Scarlett started working for Preston every night for a few hours. She not only manned the cash register, but did other odd jobs that required little energy. Marie kept Hank in the office and Scarlett enjoyed being out of the apartment.

Scarlett wasn't fond of getting to know Randy's love interests. She evaluated them and found every one inadequate for her roommate. Not that Scarlett had any right to judge, she admitted, because she certainly had less to offer Randy than any one of those women.

Randy was on the road on his birthday and since Scarlett didn't know where he was, she couldn't call him and wish him well.

But the Friday after his birthday, Randy walked into his apartment to find it decorated with balloons and streamers. He stopped abruptly when he saw the HAPPY BIRTHDAY sign spanning the wall above the sofa.

A blue and white cake with a toy truck on top was amidst plates and cups and heavy hors d'oeuvres on the table. Hank was in her carseat beside the cake. She wore a frilly pink dress no larger than a baby doll's and a minute party hat teetered on one side of her head.

Scarlett stood near the table in that same green sweater and skirt she wore for every occasion. Her hair cascaded about her like gold silk and her eyes sparkled like sunlight dancing on a forest pond. A bright smile lit up her whole face. She was beautiful.

Preston and Marie got up from the couch and Randy noticed them for the first time. He looked at their smiling faces and then back at the woman and baby.

"Well, surprise!" Scarlett finally said, laughing. Preston and Marie joined her.

Randy was at a loss for words. He'd never had a party before. What did he say? How did he act?

"I don't believe it!" Marie exclaimed. "Randy's speechless!"

Scarlett came to stand before him, reached up and removed his Stetson, then replaced it with a miniature cowboy hat. He leaned down so she could slip the rubber band under his chin.

"Happy Birthday," she said, then placed a hand on his shoulder and planted a kiss on his right cheek.

The flesh beneath her lips tingled and he wondered how the rest of his body might react to the ministrations of her full mouth. Then he shoved those thoughts from his mind.

"Don't worry," Scarlett whispered with amusement, "I didn't bake the cake."

Randy smiled.

Preston shook his hand and Marie gave him a huge bear hug as they wished him a belated happy birthday.

Randy lifted Hank from the seat and held her up for a kiss. "Hey, kid, how's it going? Did you dress up just for me?"

Hank responded with a coo and a drool.

Randy grinned and cradled her in the crook of his arm as if he'd been holding babies all his life. It amazed him how fast he'd become used to holding an infant. Only a few weeks ago he'd have been stiff. Now his arms relaxed.

"We need to light the candles and cut the cake so Preston and Marie can get to the bar," Scarlett announced.

"You aren't going to make me blow out the candles, are you?"

She nodded. "And make a wish."

Randy humored Scarlett, watching quietly as she lit all thirty candles. She stood across the table from him and met his eyes. "Go on and make a wish," she urged.

Randy wished he didn't feel this way about Scarlett. He wished he were like most of the lowdown scum he partied with who would take any woman to bed just to have a woman.

He wished he knew more about Scarlett, about her past and what role Jonas played in her life. He wanted to know what was scaring her.

And Randy wished he had the courage to ask because he knew if he pressed too hard, she'd leave. And he wished he didn't care if she left.

But the truth was he'd miss her and Hank. They kept things lively—and noisy! He liked having someone to come home to. He liked having someone to call.

There were too many selfish things for him to wish for so he wished something for Scarlett—that she'd get her life straightened out real soon.

Randy closed his eyes and blew out all thirty candles.

Scarlett and Marie cut each man a slice of cake and covered it with chocolate ice cream, then ordered them into the living room.

"So, how long are you going to be here this time?" Preston asked Randy as they settled on the couch and recliner.

"I'll be leaving on Sunday, but I'll be back on Thursday. I'll be here to take Scarlett for her six weeks' check-up."

Scarlett looked up from the half gallon of ice cream. "That's very nice of you, Randy, but isn't there something you'd rather do with your time off?"

Randy eyed her over the recliner. "Believe me, I want to."

If she only knew how much he wanted that day to get here!

Marie met Preston's eyes and winked. They seemed to be the only ones to catch the urgency in Randy's tone.

"Well, I'm anxious to get that one over with myself," Scarlett admitted.

She was anxious!

"I'm getting a little bored and when the doctor gives me my A-OK, Preston says I can be a waitress."

"Waitress?" Randy barked and choked on a cake crumb. Scarlett was beside him pounding his back to dislodge the crumb. "Sc–Sc–Scar–l–l–ett."

"What?"

"Stop pounding my back! You've dislodged the crumb, my teeth and two bones in my neck!"

Scarlett halted abruptly and crossed her arms to glare down at him.

"Is there something wrong with Scarlett being a waitress?" Marie asked as she perched on the couch arm.

Damned right there was! Short black skirts that showed too much leg! Those black skirts were meant to inspire heavy tips. They also inspired hot ideas and blazing stares. He should know, he—

He looked at the three pairs of eyes gazing at him and he knew he couldn't say he didn't want other men ogling at Scarlett's legs. Lord, Marie would have them picking out china patterns and wedding rings!

"I was wondering if it's a good idea for you to be on your feet so much, even if it will be six weeks."

Marie let out an exasperated gasp. Preston stared at him for a moment then shook his head and busied himself with his cake.

Scarlett said, "Randy, Preston's no slave driver. I think he'll let me go slow at first." Then she grinned. "Eat your cake so you can open your presents. I can't wait any longer."

Randy followed Preston's lead and kept his mouth busy with cake. Eating kept his mouth and his thoughts occupied.

I wonder if I can get seconds.

Later, when they were alone, Scarlett handed Randy a wet plate and he began to dry it. He glanced at the opened packages and shook his head. He'd never gotten so much on one occasion in his life. He knew Scarlett used most of her money to buy that silver buckle, leather belt, and book on Impressionist painting.

"Ah . . . Scarlett . . ." He set the plate on the counter. "Yes?"

"I want to thank you for all of this. No one's ever done something like this for me before."

She smiled up at him. "No one's ever done for me what you've done, Randy."

"What I did was what anyone would do for a stranger. What you did . . . well, it deserves a proper thank you."

He took her upper arms in his hands and turned her to face him. To his surprise, she didn't resist as he pulled her against him.

EIGHT

Hank's shrill cry cracked the intimate air surrounding Randy and Scarlett.

They wrenched apart like two teenagers caught petting on the porch. Their eyes swept down to Hank who wiggled in her crib on the kitchen table. She punched and kicked at the air in an exhibition of her displeasure.

Randy and Scarlett looked back at each other as their nervous laughter filled the room.

Randy shoved his hands into his back pockets, thankful Hank had the good sense to stop him. One kiss wouldn't have satisfied him.

Now, what should they do? What should they say?

Scarlett solved the dilemma by addressing Hank's tears. Catching a tiny fist in each of her hands, Scarlett patted them together. "And what's your problem, sweetie?"

Hank's mouth pursed. Her brows raised and she stared up at Scarlett with wide, wet eyes before beginning a spurt of short, distressed whines which shook her entire little body.

"Look at that tummy!" Scarlett jiggled it between her thumb and forefinger. "You can't be hungry! I bet you need changing."

"Hey," Randy said, "you need to show me how to do that."

Scarlett's eyes lifted from the blanket she was spreading on the table. "*You* want to learn to change her diaper?"

"Think it's too tough for me?"

"No, silly." She giggled. "It's just . . . well, it's not a pretty sight!"

He joined her at the table. "Woman, I've learned very little about babies is a pretty sight!"

They leaned over Hank as Scarlett lay her on the blanket then unfastened her diaper. It was soiled instead of wet.

"Have *mercy*!" Randy bolted upright.

Scarlett's lips twitched in a poor attempt to conceal her amusement.

"*That* is unbelievable!" Randy shook his head.

Scarlett shrugged. "You get used to it."

"Yeah, and the people who dispose of nuclear waste think it's a piece of cake, too!" Randy grimaced. "I don't see a lot of difference between their job and this."

Scarlett cleared her throat, but her voice still broke with laughter. "Are you sure you want to do this?"

His head bobbed up and down as he eyed the task before him. "I've done worse. I'm not sure *when*, but I'm sure I've done worse."

Under Scarlett's guidance, Randy managed to wipe and powder the baby's bottom, then secure another diaper around her without losing his cake and ice cream. In fact, the only casualty was one mangled disposable diaper.

Randy lifted Hank, feeling as if he'd just climbed the Matterhorn. "There you go, kiddo. Now, I know what to do if your mom's not around."

Scarlett's eyes clouded, threatening a full-fledged thunderstorm of tears. Randy just did something Jonas would never have done. 'That's what nannies are for,' she could hear Jonas say. She'd learned there was a lot Jonas wouldn't do that Randy would.

And, heaven help her, Scarlett almost kissed Randy!

She looked at him holding her baby. Sweet, beautiful Randy. What harm would one kiss do? Or one hug? Or one night with him?

She needed one night of tenderness and sweetness. Maybe all men had the same streak of ruthlessness, but she needed one night of the Randy he'd revealed to her thus far.

She also knew that would be the biggest mistake of her life because she no longer just worried about putting Randy's life in jeopardy. She worried about falling in love with him. Then no matter what she did, she'd lose. She could leave the man she loved or stay in town to suffer through seeing him with other women. As long as she didn't love Randy with her body, she could keep her heart in check.

"I—I'd better get ready for work," Scarlett said, checking the time.

Randy helped her bundle Hank in a thick blanket, then accompanied them to the bar. Marie took Hank as soon as they entered. Scarlett relieved the cashier at the register and Randy took possession of a stool at the end of the bar.

Preston handed him a beer and grinned. "Well, how's the birthday boy?"

"Embarrassed." Randy could feel his skin burning.

"Why?"

"Party hats? Candles? Wishes?"

Preston leaned on the bar. "Those things are nothing to be embarrassed about, boy. Especially wishes."

Randy looked over the end of the beer he'd just tipped up to his mouth and wondered where this was going. He swallowed and said, "Wishes are okay."

"Did you wish for anything?"

Randy glanced back at Scarlett. "I wished for something for her."

"You like that girl, don't you?"

Randy's head swung around to scrutinize the only man

he'd ever loved like a father. He nodded. "I like her. I like her kid. They both have spunk. But there's so much I don't know about her."

"I've been with Marie for over twenty years and she still springs new things on me. I think that's why I stick around. She's never dull."

"Well, I can sure say that about Scarlett!" Randy laughed and shook his head. "A birthday party for me!"

Preston looked deep into Randy's eyes and said, "I love you like you were my flesh and blood son, so I'm going to say this only once then I'll leave you alone."

Randy stifled a groan.

"I know how you feel about love and commitment and all that. And I know that girl is a mystery to you. One thing that ain't a mystery is she's definitely scared of something. To take on Scarlett and Hank full-time might be one of the most frustrating, dangerous things a person could do. And I'm not saying you should."

"But?" Randy said.

"But I have seen the two of you together and there are some damned bright sparks snapping between the two of you. And I'm not just talking sex." His look squelched any lewd comment Randy might make, although he wasn't going to say a word. "Well, what I'm leading up to is this—where women are concerned there are no rules of thumb. You follow your heart because when a woman's involved that's the only male organ with any sense."

Then he gave Randy an example. "Don't waste time with tarts when you could have a whole apple pie." He raised his hands. "I won't say anymore."

"Hey, Randy."

It took Randy a second to shift his attention to the man who had joined him. "Hey, Mr. Foster. How are you?"

Denby Foster was the community's eccentric millionaire. No one knew how much money he had—even Denby. He was a nice old guy who lived in a modest home about five miles north of Dominion. He would give the shirt off his back to someone in need. It was a good thing Denby lived in Dominion where the citizens wouldn't think of taking advantage of him because Denby's IQ wasn't nearly as bountiful as his generous nature and abundant funds.

"I'm fine. How are you?" the old man returned.

"Oh, I can't complain." Actually, Randy could complain since he just noticed Scarlett was talking to a cowboy he didn't recognize. A twinge of jealousy that the cowboy was being treated to Scarlett's raspy voice and green gaze nagged him.

"That's a nice rig you have," Denby mentioned.

"Well, thank you. It's not the Mercedes of trucks, but it serves my purpose."

"Oh, I like it. I like it so much I tried to buy one exactly like it."

"You did?"

Denby gave him an affirmative shake of his head and scratched the two day's growth of beard on his chin. "But to get one *exactly* like yours would take me four months!"

"That so?" Randy looked back at Scarlett. That cowboy was hitting on her for sure.

"So, I'll give you one hundred thousand dollars for yours."

That caught Randy's attention. "Say what?"

"One hundred thousand in cash."

The offer was tempting. Mighty tempting. Randy could live very well on one hundred thousand, but that was what he'd saved over the years to buy this rig. Trucking was in his blood and he had to do it. If it took Denby four months to get a truck, it would take him that long, too. He wouldn't be able to live off the money and pay for the truck all at the same time.

But, aside from that, Denby was a fancier. What he fancied, he bought. He now owned an army surplus Jeep, a trolley car, and a one-man submarine.

The problem was Denby's interest soon faded and the

objects of his fancy died slow deaths from the elements. Randy wasn't about to let *his* truck disintegrate from lack of use.

"Well, I appreciate the offer, Mr. Foster, but I think I'll hang onto my truck for awhile longer." *I'm a fool.*

Denby sighed. "Well, I guess I can understand that. But you keep in mind my offer. Okay?"

Randy turned back to Scarlett to find her smile had faded. The cowboy now barred the only exit from behind the counter. Scarlett looked worried.

"Okay," Randy answered Denby, but rose from the barstool, ready to spring to Scarlett's aid. Then she pointed toward him. The cowboy swung around and squinted through the smoke at Randy. He nodded in greeting, but didn't smile as he waited to see what would happen. The cowboy said something to Scarlett and left. Randy relaxed and settled back onto the stool.

"Well, looky here, boys."

Randy turned his head and smiled. His three poker buddies had replaced Denby, who'd moved on down the bar. Randy felt a little guilty for ignoring the old man. "Hello, boys."

After they all greeted each other and ordered another round of beers, they settled into some man talk.

They discussed sports, Randy's travels, and what had happened since they were all together last.

Larry, who was so thin his mustache outweighed him, asked, "Hey, when are we going to have another poker game?"

"Yeah," Ted agreed as he pushed aside the shock of blond hair which forever crept into his blue eyes. "We need to have another poker game."

"Of course, our homes have been made off limits to poker games by our wives," Russell pointed out.

Randy took the hint from his red-haired, bearded friend who resembled a slovenly Viking. "You know you can have it at my place."

"Well, we didn't know if Scarlett would mind."

"Why would she mind? You come over Friday night at seven and bring your own beer."

Once they left, Randy looked back at Scarlett, studied her for a moment, then motioned to Preston to lean across the bar. "Mind taking the cash register for Scarlett? I'd like to dance."

Preston shook his head. "No, there are too many bartenders back here anyway."

They walked over to Scarlett who crossed her arms and said, "When the two of you are together, it can only mean trouble."

"I wanted to dance with you and Preston offered to take the register."

Scarlett eyed the dancers gliding about the parquet floor and hesitated. "I don't dance very well to this music."

"Neither do they." Randy extended his hand. "Come on. I'll teach you."

Once on the dance floor, Scarlett admitted, "I don't dance very well at all."

"Don't worry. You'll do fine," Randy assured her.

It took only a few moments to teach Scarlett the fundamentals of the Texas Swing. She looked up at him and exclaimed, "This is fun!"

"You're doing fine for someone who doesn't dance very well."

"Well, I never had a lot of chances to dance."

His head tilted in disbelief. "I can't believe boys never asked you to dance."

"They didn't. I was all legs and teeth and freckles."

Randy couldn't imagine any red-blooded male minding legs that could wrap about him. He moved further away from her. His thoughts worked on his body with a vengeance.

He changed the subject. "So, what did that cowboy want?"

"A one-night stand."

"What did you say to get rid of him?"

Scarlett looked up at him, sheepishly, color staining her cheeks. "I, uh, told him he'd have to ask my baby's father."

Randy should have felt a thousand things other than the pride swelling up within him. He felt like Hank's father, the only father she'd ever known, anyway. Then he reminded himself, Scarlett just used that line to get rid of a womanizing cowboy—a carbon copy of himself.

"I hope this doesn't offend any of your girlfriends," Scarlett said, glancing about for any watchful eyes and poised weapons.

"They're not my girlfriends."

"Well, they think they are. You are really a popular fellow, Randy Taylor. Look at that flock of good-ol'-boys who joined you awhile ago at the bar."

"One wanted to buy my truck. The other three were setting up a poker game with me."

Scarlett stiffened, then stopped dancing all together. Randy looked down into accusing, hurt green eyes. "What's wrong?"

She didn't say anything, couldn't say anything. Her head throbbed and her heart pounded. So these were Randy's true colors. A *gambler*! She wrenched free of him and ran to the office.

Confused and embarrassed, Randy scanned the crowd to see if anyone noticed he'd been stranded, then he followed her. Marie, seeing their serious expressions, sensed they wanted to be alone and left. Randy never saw her leave, his eyes were fixed upon Scarlett's back. She stood over Hank, staring down at the baby, refusing to acknowledge the man who stood behind her.

"Scarlett?"

She ignored him.

"What happened out there?" The silence drove him crazy. He swung her around, careful not to jerk her too hard and yet enough to let her know he wanted an answer.

"Tell me, for heaven's sake! For once, trust me enough to tell me *something*!"

Tears glittered in her eyes and clung to her long lashes. She suddenly blurted, "Poker! Gambling!"

Randy released her, angry that she was suddenly dictating what he could and couldn't do with his life. "That's what this is about? A friendly game of poker? Scarlett, it's just a game and some time with the guys. I'd give you the world if I could, but I won't be henpecked."

"My father was a gambler!" she blurted, her tears giving her voice a desperate edge. "It was a disease. He gambled away everything we had until we were forced to live in a shack in the desert and it killed my mother!"

Randy could do nothing but look at her. He couldn't breathe. He couldn't think. He just stared. For weeks, she'd given him nothing of herself and now it rushed forth like a swollen creek. He didn't like what he'd learned. It shocked him. It hurt him. It made him hurt for her.

She swallowed and closed her eyes, then opened them and gazed into space. "He still gambled and I still loved him. Like a fool, I still loved him. I even loved him after he asked me to sell my soul to the devil."

The devil?! Rage burned through Randy. What had the man done to make Scarlett's life such a turmoil? Randy wanted to give him a taste of his own medicine; inflict slow, lengthy pain.

But Scarlett didn't need his seeking revenge right now. She needed his comfort.

She'd turned back to Hank and scooped the child into her arms. Randy stepped close to her, his chest touching her back. She trembled against him and then melted.

"Scarlett."

She didn't answer.

"Scarlett," he repeated.

"I—I'm sorry. I shouldn't have blown up at you like that."

"Hey." He gently turned her to him. "Come here."

A long sigh escaped from Scarlett when he pulled her and Hank into his arms, encompassing them in his strength and warmth.

Scarlett leaned against him with a desperation that tightened his throat and made seeking vengeance that much harder to brush aside. Then she cried.

He let her cry, smoothing her hair and whispering soothing words. Her tears soaked his plaid shirt. Her body jerked convulsively as long-suppressed tears rushed from her. She'd cried a lot in the last few weeks, but these sobs were the release of years of pain.

"I'm just an emotional time bomb!" she confessed. "It wasn't that bad . . . I exaggerated."

"I don't think so," Randy said. "I think it was just as painful as it sounded."

Scarlett nodded.

"I'm sorry."

Scarlett looked up at him. "You really mean it, don't you?"

"Yes."

"Why are you so good to me? You've known me only a month and yet you've done more for me than my father or—or anyone."

Randy brushed away a tear from her cheek with his thumb and answered, "I honestly don't know."

She managed a smile.

"Your father had a disease. I don't. I planned a poker game for next Friday night and that's all it is—a game. But if it upsets you, I'll cancel it."

She shook her head. "No. I overreacted. I'm sorry. I didn't mean to sound as if I was telling you what to do. Have your poker game and have fun with your friends."

Randy wanted to tell her she could request anything and he'd try to do it. The demanding was what irked him. He needed to make her feel protected and secure and yet he wondered if words would be enough. It was worth a try.

"Scarlett, whatever those men did to you will never happen again. I promise."

Scarlett almost believed him. She really wanted to believe him, but that same sincere look in his eyes right now was just a rerun of what she'd seen in her father's and in Jonas's more times than she cared to count.

Maybe Randy meant what he said. But he'd just made a promise he could never keep. He'd forget that vow if Jonas ever confronted him. Until that time came—as long as she guarded herself and knew what to expect—what harm could it do to accept what he offered?

Later, much later, Randy stretched out on the couch and stared at the shadows playing on the ceiling. Had Scarlett been too emotionally worked up to catch his declaration that he'd give her the world if he could? Or had she just chosen to ignore it? And was she glad or disappointed? Damned if he knew. He didn't understand much about himself these days, least of all the things he was feeling about Scarlett Kincaid.

Randy hated to leave on Sunday. Scarlett had been unusually quiet the whole weekend, although she insisted she was fine. He had an ominous feeling she'd be gone when he returned on Thursday so he called her every night. Her picking up the phone each time filled him with an overwhelming sense of relief.

Each day, her spirits seemed higher and he felt encouraged, but he steeled himself to find an empty apartment upon his return.

The last few miles of his trip were torture. He alternated between driving overly slow to avoid the inevitable, and speeding in an effort to face the truth and begin to rebuild his life. He wondered if he *could* rebuild his life and that doubt scared him.

Even the light in the window didn't convince him Scarlett was still there. As he took the steps two at a time, he considered she might be cruel and leave a light on to fool him. When he opened the door, however, and found her wearing the black slacks and white blouse for her job at Preston's, he gave an audible sigh of relief.

"Glad to be home?" Scarlett asked, giving him a welcoming smile.

"Something like that."

"Randy's home, baby." Scarlett lifted Hank and came closer to Randy, holding the baby up so she could focus upon him. "See?"

He cupped a hand on the top of Hank's curly head and she gazed up at him. "Hey, kiddo." He leaned down and gave her an exaggerated kiss. As he raised his head, he contemplated and decided against kissing her mother.

"You're going to work?"

She nodded. "You want to come along?"

"Nah," he said, "I'm tired. I think I'll stay around here tonight. Maybe go on to bed."

But after she left, Randy became restless. He had a sneaking suspicion what was causing this feeling, but he refused to face it. Instead, he pulled out his drawing materials and sat down at the table to work off his tension by being creative.

An hour later, he had a finished sketch of Scarlett nursing Hank. He sat back, blinking at the paper before him. It hadn't even occurred to him what he was doing until he made the final stroke of the charcoal and he was thinking how he'd like to put it on canvas in soft, muted hues.

Randy shoved the drawing into the bottom drawer of his dresser and went to bed.

Friday, Randy took Scarlett and Hank for their checkups. To his relief, they were both healthy. He wished they were going to celebrate properly instead of his playing poker with the boys.

Mid-afternoon the phone rang and Scarlett answered it. When she hung up, she sat on the sofa and met Randy's eyes tentatively. "That was Marie. She has a bad cold and won't be at the bar tonight . . . I don't have a babysitter."

Randy's gaze left the ballgame and met Scarlett's.

"I don't know what to do with Hannah."

Randy envisioned four hairy-legged, beer-guzzling men carrying on a poker game between diaper changes and feedings. What a thought!

But he found himself saying, "I'll keep her tonight."

Scarlett eyed him. "*You*?"

"Sure. But what about feeding her?"

"She's almost weaned, but I'll feed her before I leave and I'll put a relief bottle in the refrigerator."

Relief bottle. Randy knew them well. There was nothing like reaching into the refrigerator for a cold beer and wrapping your hand around a warm container of breast milk. No sirree. Nothing like it. Randy blushed.

Scarlett smiled, then asked, "Are you sure you don't mind babysitting?"

"I'm sure. How much trouble can she be?"

Scarlett left at six-thirty. At six-thirty-one Hank began to cry. Randy picked her up and she stopped. He bounced her for awhile and her eyes began to close, so he lay her in her drawer.

He opened a bag of chips, unscrewed the top from a jar of Spanish olives, and was reaching for a container of dip when Hank's cries broke out again. He let her cry.

He let her cry for ten minutes.

Then his nerves could take no more.

Randy juggled the infant in one arm and with his free hand, he set up the poker game and moved the food to a TV table nearby. *Huh! There's nothing to this babysitting stuff.*

When the knock on the door came, Randy looked down at Hank. Her eyes teared and her lips quivered just as if she knew he was going to put her down. He sighed and opened the door.

Larry, Russell, and Ted filled the doorway, beer in hand

and smiles on their faces. Their eyes dropped collectively to Hank and their smiles left their faces.

"Well, if this don't beat all I've ever seen," Russell said.

Until that point no one had spoken. They'd all sat down at the table, pulled the tabs on some beers, and Ted dealt out a game of five-card stud. No *words* were spoken, but Randy could almost hear the jaws working and the mental cogs grinding as the three men fumed. Everyone knew that even though Hank was a baby, she'd still put a damper on the good spirits of the game.

Randy, across the table from Russell, held his cards with one hand and cradled Hank in the crook of his free arm.

"I don't know which is more unbelievable. Us being part of four men and a baby, or seeing Randy Taylor with an infant."

Randy didn't know either. He wished someone had a camera so he could see just how foolish he really looked, but he wasn't about to confess that to these guys.

"Are you going to play cards or run off at the mouth, Russell?" he asked lightly.

Russell's meaty face broke into a good-natured grin. "I'm going to *win* the poker game, not just play it."

"Yeah, well put your money where your mouth is because I can beat you with one arm wrapped around a baby."

Ted lit up a cigar and blew heavy smoke across the table. Randy glared at him then inclined his head toward Hank. Ted glanced at the other two men, who offered him noncommittal shrugs. He stubbed out the cigar.

After a few hands, they took a refreshment break and Larry ambled to the refrigerator to replenish everyone's brew.

"How 'bout a bottle for the lady?" he asked, lifting the relief bottle.

Randy nodded, not daring to tell him what *kind* of milk sloshed inside the glass container. Larry was more bashful about that sort of thing than Randy and he'd fathered four kids.

Hank had discovered she could stuff all four fingers into her mouth and objected loudly when Randy pulled her hand from her lips. He offered her the nipple of the bottle, but she jerked her head away. He couldn't blame her. It couldn't compare to her mama's.

Awhile later, they took a break to rummage through the refrigerator for food. Randy cleared the table.

"Hey," Russell said, wagging a fried chicken leg at Randy. "Whatcha doing?"

"She needs changing."

"Don't tell me you do that, too?" Russell questioned, his face paling behind his red beard.

"I'll be in the bathroom," Larry announced. "Let me know when it's over."

"Hell, Randy," Russell stomped to his side, waving his hand and the molested chicken leg in the air. "We don't even change our own kids."

"Maybe you should," Randy told them, pulling at the tapes of Hank's diaper and slipping it off her bottom. Unconcerned with her nakedness or the men watching her, Hank curled up her legs and gurgled. She busied herself with the examination of her right hand.

Russell and Ted watched in disgust as their womanizing hero ran through the procedure of powdering the baby's bottom and replacing the wet diaper with a dry pink one.

Their eyes widened with horror as Randy jiggled the baby's stomach and murmured the language only those who love babies can speak or translate.

Then Hank smiled.

It took Randy by surprise. He'd never seen her do that before. It lasted only a few seconds, but there was no doubting he'd just been blessed with the most adorable, toothless baby grin ever witnessed by mankind.

"Did you see that?" he asked Russell. "She smiled!"

Russell's expression clearly stated he questioned Randy's mental capacity at this moment. "Yeah, Randy, we saw it." He elbowed Ted who stood beside him.

"Yeah, Randy," Ted added as if Randy were a crazed maniac to be appeased. "Real cute."

Randy eyed one man, then the other. Well, they thought an alien possessed his body. Maybe one did. He wasn't going to waste his time trying to convert these guys to the joys of fatherhood when it was obvious Scarlett would be the only one to appreciate this moment.

He picked up Hank. "Put the stuff back on the table, get Larry out of the bathroom, and let's get on with the game."

"Hey, Randy, we didn't—"

Russell's apology died in Randy's bright-blue glare.

The bearded giant shuffled to the bathroom, retrieved Larry, and everyone sat down in unison. A few minutes of silent card playing broke Russell's reserves. He tossed his cards into the middle of the table. "Hell, Randy, we didn't mean to hurt your feelings."

"We sure didn't," Ted agreed.

Randy's eyes shifted from Russell to Ted, but he said nothing.

Russell continued, "It's just that you ain't been yourself lately, and we don't know what to think of it."

"What do you mean I've not been myself?" Randy asked with a short laugh.

Russell and Ted met each other's worried eyes then looked at Randy. It was Russell who became the spokesman. "You take a woman and a baby into your apartment. You hardly ever show up at Preston's. This is the first poker game in seven weeks. Hell, Randy, you ain't even been to the hunting lodge once."

"I've been on the road, guys. I don't have a lot of time for drinking, card playing, and going to the lodge. Besides, hunting season's over."

Realizing Hank was in a deep sleep at last, he got up and took her to the drawer they'd placed on the couch. "As far as taking a woman and baby into the apartment, what did you expect me to do? Leave them on the side of the road?"

Russell shook his head and waved his hand. "No, no. We didn't mean that."

Coming back to the table, hands in his pockets and an interrogating gleam in his eyes, Randy asked, "What did you mean, Russell? Spit it out."

Russell hesitated, then sighed. "We think Scarlett's a fine woman . . ."

"But."

"But, you ain't been out with a woman since she came along."

"You've been spying on me?" Randy glared at Russell, then Ted and Larry. All three glowed with the heat of embarrassment.

"I wouldn't call it spying," Ted tried to explain.

"Well, Ted," Randy said, dropping onto his chair and placing his elbows on the table. "What would you call it?"

"Following your career?"

"My what?" Randy leaned back against the chair in disbelief.

Russell told him, "You know, Randy, we've all looked up to you."

"Why would you possibly look up to me?"

"Because we got snared into the marriage trap and you're still free. We always liked to hear the details of your life, because it kept us linked to things our wives would kill us for if we did them."

Ted and Larry agreed with a nod.

Randy picked up a poker chip and studied it. "Well, your hero worship is misplaced."

"Not when you were telling us about your love life," Ted told him.

"I sure did love to hear the stories." Larry grinned.

Outside, Scarlett reached the landing only to hear voices. Tired, she felt a surge of disappointment that the poker game was still going on. She didn't want to barge in on the boys, but she sure needed a hot bath and a place to prop her feet. She leaned her forehead against the door as she decided between invading male territory or going back downstairs to wait at the bar.

Inside, Russell said, "You ain't told us one thing about Scarlett."

"Yeah, Randy," Ted leaned forward, "How *are* you and the little lady getting along?"

Scarlett pressed her ear to the door. What would Randy say? Would he be a snake in the grass and make up some kind of outlandish story about the wild times spent with his roomie behind closed doors? He could, because he had no idea she stood outside the door, listening, waiting to see if he'd sacrifice his reputation or confirm the one Dominion had manufactured for her.

"Which little lady?" Randy asked after a moment. "The twenty-five-year old or the six-week old?"

The men groaned.

"Tell us *something*, Randy," Larry pleaded. "You always have before."

Scarlett stiffened, expecting Randy's next words to prove her fears that he was like every man in her life—a real slime bag.

Randy met each of his friend's eyes and, after a long pause, he admitted, "There's nothing to tell. We're just roommates."

Three chairs scraped away from the table in unison. Randy's friends all commented at once. In Scarlett's stunned daze, she heard words like "reputation" and "Casanova" mixed with lots of laughter. They were making fun of Randy.

She'd expected the worst from Randy . . . again. Once

again, he'd disappointed her—or pleased her. Damn! She didn't know what he did to her anymore!

One thing was for sure, his friends thought he'd lost his touch or gone soft on them. They wouldn't keep their mouths shut and Randy's reputation would be ruined before the sun rose tomorrow morning.

Some friends.

Scarlett suddenly realized she didn't care about her reputation. She'd be gone from this town in a few weeks, so what did it matter what people thought of her? Randy had to live here. He'd placed himself in a position to be ridiculed for her and she had to repay him, to set the score right somehow.

Then an idea came to her.

Scarlett twisted the knob, bolted through the door and announced, "Hey, babe, I'm home!"

Scarlett could feel the shocked reactions of the men in the room, but, keeping her eyes on Randy, she could only see the puzzlement on his face.

She sashayed to the table where he sat and plopped onto his lap, and one of his hands splayed against her spine out of its own volition.

"I sure missed you tonight," Scarlett said, pushing back a stray swath of his dark curly hair to reveal his furrowed brow.

Randy opened his mouth to speak. He wanted to ask what the hell she thought she was doing.

He never got the chance because Scarlett's mouth swooped down upon his in a fiery, devouring kiss.

NINE

The kiss seemed to last forever.

Even thinking about beets didn't diminish the effects Scarlett's lips inflicted upon Randy's body this time. So he gave up the fight.

Randy's arms slipped about her, pulling her against him. His tongue plunged to meet hers, to caress it and tease it. God, she tasted good!

Scarlett's hands slithered up the strong column of his neck and dipped into the chestnut curls on the back of his head. A path of electricity arced between her fingers and his skin.

Their lips gnawed at each other. Their tongues curled together in an erotic mating dance. Their breaths, escaping in short spurts, became one inside the hollow of their mouths.

Then Scarlett eased away from Randy in a slow, fluid movement that ripped the air from his lungs.

The soft swell of her bosom rose and fell rapidly against his chest. Her lips glistened. Her lids hung heavy over her eyes.

Randy looked into Scarlett's eyes and wondered if her sudden startled expression reflected his own. This kiss had been a bad idea because it affected them in ways neither wanted to address. They'd nearly kissed before, but until the actual act, they could shove aside their feelings.

It was also a bad idea because he wanted to kiss her again and again, exclusively and forever, and he didn't like those implications.

Russell's nervous cough brought their gazes to him. Scarlett smiled politely. She knew the three men from the bar. They were regulars and she'd exchanged a few words with them on occasion.

"Hello, Russell. Ted. Larry."

"Hey, Scarlett," they said in unison.

"Did I break up the poker game?"

"No . . . no," Russell told her, "In fact, the boys and I were just getting ready to call it a night. Weren't we?"

He elbowed Ted who added, "We sure were. Come on, Larry."

"We'll have to do this again real soon," Randy suggested.

The three men uttered noncommittal comments and shuffled out the door.

As soon as the door clicked behind the three men, Randy and Scarlett looked at each other, trying to read the other's thoughts.

The kiss was a bad idea. Scarlett saw the odd way Randy stared at her. She'd made him mad. In her effort to save his reputation, she'd probably ruined it by such a display in front of his friends.

"Scarlett, let me up."

She obeyed, stunned by the seriousness in his voice. She'd seldom seen him in any state except happy or angry. This was a quiet, controlled condition, and she didn't like it.

Her stomach churned as she watched him collect his hat and coat and head for the door. "Wh-where are you going?"

He pulled on his coat. "Out."

"Randy," Scarlett said as she took a step toward him. "I'm sorry. I didn't mean to make you mad."

He stared at her for a long time. Those pale eyes held her in their gaze and made her uneasy, though not necessarily in a bad way.

He walked to her, slipping his cool fingers along the heated flesh on the back of her neck. His lips claimed hers in a quick, but deep kiss. With his mouth just above hers, he whispered, "Hank smiled tonight." On that positive note, he walked out of the apartment.

Scarlett stared at the door for a long time, her fingers pressed against the flesh still tingling from Randy's kiss.

"Dixie, are you out there?"

Randy didn't know if she was anywhere in the area, but he sure could use her friendly voice. So he'd called her for the last fifteen minutes—about ten longer than he'd normally try.

Dixie's slow drawl skimmed across the airwaves. "What? No Breaker one–nine?"

"Sorry."

"Hey, is this Lone Star or some bad impostor?"

Randy sighed. Even separated by airwaves Dixie was tuned into his moods. "I guess I've got a lot on my mind."

Dixie grunted. "Tell me about it! My kid sister is a living nightmare. I knew there was a reason I moved out before she was old enough to talk!"

That made Randy smile. He recalled the day about a year ago when Dixie received custody of the "Kid Sister from Hell." Their mother had died and Dixie became guardian of Johnnie at the worst possible time—the beginning of her adolescence.

"But what's bothering *you*, Star?"

As if he had to tell her. Her tone told him she knew.

"Do I have to say it?" he asked quietly.

"No," she said, serious for a change. "I guess you don't. Star . . . do you love her?"

Randy stared out over the moonlit field where he'd parked his pickup truck. The pointed question stabbed him right in the gut. He might have subconsciously thought about it, but the spoken words had him trembling in his boots. "I don't know, Dix."

"What do you mean, you don't know? Get real, Star."

"I know nothing about her, Dixie."

"That's not what I asked. You know what you need to know. Now, do you love her or not?"

Dammit! Why did she have to insist on things being so cut and dried? They weren't. If he evaded the question, this issue might just go away.

But it wouldn't go away.

Yes, he loved Scarlett. Now and forever.

That revelation threw his equilibrium into a tailspin. Admitting it to himself was more than enough for one day, but he knew Dixie would never quit until she pulled the truth from him—unless he did some smooth talking. "I have never loved anyone in my life, Dix. That's why I called myself Lone Star."

"You don't have to have experience for this, you oaf. This is an intimate relationship we're talking about, not a job interview."

"But . . ."

Dixie lost her patience. "But what, you idiot? Are you worried about your stupid reputation as a womanizer? We both know that it's a bunch of bull!"

A bunch of bull? She'd teased him all this time, and she knew the truth?

Before he could recover and ask her how she knew, she answered him.

"I don't have to be face to face with you to know you're not that kind of man. But even if you were, you can't live forever like that. One of these days you'll be pot-bellied and bald, and no woman is going to leap at chance to be with you . . . Except a woman who really loves you.''

Dixie gave him a moment to digest her words then continued. ''You aren't committing a crime if you love someone, Star. You won't see your picture in the post office.''

No. That was true. But he sure could see his heart on the chopping block and Scarlett with an ax in her hand. All the years of self-reliance had built a pretty steep wall about him, much as he hated to admit it. He'd never considered loving someone before because it would give too much control over his life to another human being.

They were talking love here. Not lust that could burn itself out like a wildfire given enough time. *Love*. Through thick and thin. For better or worse. It meant accepting Hank as his own child. It meant—Lord have mercy— china patterns and wedding rings!

It meant forever.

He didn't have to make that commitment, by George. He could go on with life just the way it'd always been. No . . . not the way it'd always been. Now, there'd be memories and feelings marring his happiness. Randy found that alternative unacceptable.

''Yeah, Dixie, I love her,'' he said, surprised at the relief that flooded over him.

''Then I suggest you go home and tell the woman. It can't be any worse than what you've put yourself through for the last six weeks.''

Before he could say anymore, Dixie ten-foured off the air.

Scarlett sat in the darkness, her legs curled beneath her. She stared at the door. She didn't know how long she'd been that way.

She should have left. The winter weather had moved on, if only for a short time. Though nippy outside, it wouldn't be a threat to her or Hannah's health.

Things were getting too heated between Scarlett and Randy. She was no fool. She could see things were different with him than with any other man she'd ever known. She could truly love this man, and that scared her because Jonas would haunt her until his dying day. That haunting included ruining anyone she loved.

She knew Randy well enough to know he'd want to fight Jonas, which was impossible. One thing and one thing only could fight her ex-husband—money and lots of it.

Neither she nor Randy had enough money to fill a coffee cup, let alone stand up to a powerful millionaire.

So, she ought to leave.

But she just wasn't ready to leave. She let out a small laugh and shook her head. If she waited until she was ready, she'd be too old to make an exit.

Scarlett was deep in her thoughts when Randy unlocked the door, and she didn't even notice he'd returned until he stepped inside the warm apartment. Startled, her eyes met his and they both froze in silent appraisal of each other.

Randy finally closed the door and removed his hat and coat. Scarlett watched him walk to the refrigerator and pour a glass of orange juice. As he gulped the contents of the glass, she rummaged through her mind for the exact words to make things right between them. Would it be better for him to remain angry with her? It might be easier to leave if he were. Or should she try to patch up their friendship?

Randy finished his juice, washed out the glass and placed it on the counter, then turned to look at Scarlett again. God, she was beautiful. His body filled with love for her. His body filled with need for her.

She stood and walked toward him. He helped her close the distance between them.

"Randy—"

He covered her opened mouth with his, cupping her face

in his hands. Her words were lost in the sweet comfort of his kiss. His hands pushed up through her hair and skimmed down her back to pull her close to him.

Scarlett didn't want to think. If she thought, she'd stop this and it felt too good . . . way too good. She just wanted to react to all the wonderful things happening to her right now.

Randy's mouth captured hers in an erotic ritual of tugs, gnaws, and presses. His hands spread against her spine and slid up the curve of her back until he reached her shoulders. Desire surged from him in an electrifying jolt and he pulled her against the long, hard length of him. Soft, feminine inch matched to solid, masculine inch. Denim to pink sweatpants.

The quivering muscles of Scarlett's abdomen worked like flint striking steel, igniting a spark which immediately became a fireball of burning need raging over her entire body. She became pliant in his hands, clinging to him as her knees weakened. Her mind cleared of everything but Randy and his wonderful lips. His firm, warm, sensual mouth.

And then his mouth left hers. His hands slipped up her shoulders to her neck and cupped her face once more.

Scarlett's eyes popped open. What the *hell* was he doing? He couldn't possibly be having second thoughts . . . Could he? Not *now*! Not when she was so worked up. When she wanted more of him. Needed more. Had to have more.

Scarlett flung her arms about Randy's neck. Her weight sent him staggering back a step. Air left his lungs in a loud 'oompf' that was muffled by her mouth rubbing hungrily over his.

Randy circled an arm about her waist and spread his feet to counterbalance her. The move did nothing to stabilize his senses, however.

He pulled away a little. "Scarlett . . . I . . . I want you." *I love you*. Dammit! Why couldn't he just say it?!

Scarlett looked up at him. She should say no. She should run for the hills. How could she ever leave him if she didn't say no? "I want you, too," she said, breathlessly.

Randy eliminated the distance between them. His tongue traced her lips. They eagerly parted, allowing him to explore the wet, smooth cavern of her mouth. Was this a preview of what was to come? He groaned with anticipation, pulling her closer, his hands pushing up her sweatshirt until nothing separated him from her full breasts. Her nipples beaded under the gentle kneading of his thumbs. She whimpered with pleasure.

Every thread of Randy's clothing became unbearable as weeks of abstinence collected into a throbbing ache beneath his zipper. His hands dropped, cupping her buttocks. He nudged his hips against hers. The move only intensified the sweet tension building within him, magnifying it until he felt like a pressure cooker with a stuck valve.

Randy needed to get her to bed. Fast.

He scooped Scarlett into his arms and headed for the bedroom. His mouth fused to hers, he relied on instinct to guide him.

Scarlett's fingers twisted in the hair behind his ears. She planted huge, exaggerated kisses on his mouth and moved down the length of his neck and up to his jaw.

She refused to release her hold on him when he placed her in the middle of the fluffy, red comforter on his bed.

"Scarlett, you have to let me go."

"No. I don't want you to go. Even for a second."

His eyes blazed with joy over her open display of desire. His hands pressed on either side of her to steady himself. "Honey, there are two things this man has never done and doesn't intend to start now. One is chew tobacco." A brown brow cocked upward. "The other is make love with my boots on."

Scarlett remembered she wore no shoes, but Randy wasn't as lucky. She giggled and rested her arms on the pillow over her head, lazing like a cat in the sun as she watched Randy.

He removed his boots and began to strip off his shirt. The sight of her, legs rubbing against each other, breasts jutting upward, unnerved him. His buttons torpedoed across the room in his haste to join her. His pants followed his shirt to make a heap on the floor. With a heavy sigh, he stretched out beside her.

Scarlett's fingers combed through the thick pelt curling over his chest as if admiring an expensive fur coat. Her palms covered his pectorals, rubbing and pressing until his nipples were pebbles against her hands.

Their lips brushed, then possessed each other hungrily. Their tongues collided in blundering urgency, backed off, then plunged forth to curl around each other.

Sweet. She's so sweet.

Impatiently, Randy undressed her and the pink sweatsuit met the same fate as his clothes. He licked at the sexy little mole between her breasts then moved to lap at one of her mounds of creamy flesh. "You're so beautiful," he murmured, his hot breath forming steamy, moist circles on her skin.

Scarlett gasped.

"Touch me," he whispered.

She touched him, closing about him, stroking him until he groaned with pain and pleasure.

He pulled her hand away. "On second thought, if you continue that, I won't last through this."

"You'd better make it through this. Do you know what a sexually starved woman can do?"

His head tilted back and he closed his eyes as she sought him again. *Torture. Blessed torture.* "No," he ground out through clenched teeth. "But you're about to see what a sexually frustrated man will do if you don't stop that."

She stilled beneath him. "You? Sexually frustrated?"

He reached between their bodies, grabbed her hands and pinned them above her head. "Yes!" He gave her a quick kiss, then brought a hand down to caress her face. "Scarlett, I haven't been with anyone since you came into my life."

Scarlett gawked at him, but her questions were blown into oblivion as his hand trailed over her body—down the valley between her breasts, over her almost-flat stomach, and ended at the womanly mound between her thighs. "Randy!" she cried.

Enough. She was ready. He'd been ready a long time. No more waiting.

He reached across her to search through the nightstand drawer. He raised a foil pack before her glazed green eyes. "We don't want any more Hanks right now."

A moment later, he covered her with his body and she guided him into position. He slid into her with one long, fluid thrust. As she arched up, he murmured into her ear, "Scarlett . . . I love you."

Scarlett didn't know if his body or his words touched her inner core, but she knew this was no longer a man she *could* love. This was the man she loved.

She rose to meet his every thrust. She wrapped herself about him, arms and legs, drawing him further and further within her until there was nowhere to go. He'd joined her soul.

Randy groaned and gathered her to him.

A tear glided down Scarlett's cheek as Randy thrust one last time and they jumped into the white-hot flames of their desire.

Randy didn't move for a long time. He didn't know how long he remained enveloped inside Scarlett, the rippling aftershocks of her climax caressing him. He might have fallen asleep for awhile, but he wasn't sure.

Awareness of what was going on around him returned with the gentle strokes of Scarlett's fingers up and down his back. Her body was perfectly still beneath him.

Randy raised himself on his elbows and smiled down at her. "O-o-oh, Lordy, Miss Scarlett!"

Scarlett returned his smile, her hands resting on the small of his back. Her eyes glowed.

He leaned down and kissed her. "I'll be right back."

As Randy left the room, a thousand emotions stirred within her. Fear. Surprise. The need for reassurance. She felt like an exposed nerve.

Too keyed up to wait complacently on the bed, Scarlett decided to get up. She flung back the covers and gasped as the cool night air tortured her naked body. Opening one of the dresser drawers, she pulled out a large white fisherman's knit sweater and tugged it over her head. Something fell against her foot and she jumped back a step, her heart racing.

In the moonlight, Scarlett could see a piece of paper on the floor and picked it up. She reached for the lamp switch by the bed and had to sit down when she saw what she held.

It was a charcoal drawing of her nursing Hank, the likeness so uncanny she could hardly breathe. Yet, there was something unreal, unnatural about the rendition.

Purity.

The woman in that drawing was pure.

Scarlett knew Randy was the artist. Was that how he really pictured her? Pure?

Well, she sure didn't feel pure. She felt tarnished, ruined. A cry caught in her throat and she covered her mouth with a trembling hand.

"Scarlett."

Startled, Scarlett's eyes lifted and she tossed the paper onto the bed. "R–Randy, I'm sorry. I wasn't snooping. I–I was just l–looking for a sweater."

He knelt in front of her, taking her hands in his. "I don't care. I would have shown it to you eventually . . . Why are you crying? And don't tell me my artistic talent moved you to tears."

A faint smile touched her lips as a tear rolled down her cheek.

"What's wrong, babe?"

She hesitated. Once she began, she'd have to tell it all and she'd told no one the truth—not the whole truth. "You said you loved me."

"I know and I meant it."

"But you shouldn't. Love me, I mean."

He frowned. "Why not?"

"You know nothing about me."

Randy pulled himself up to sit beside her. "So, tell me something. You *can* trust me, you know."

The slight tension in his voice brought her eyes up to his. Yes, she owed him the truth. She owed him her trust. "I trust you with my life . . . with Hannah's life. It's *your* life I don't trust in *my* hands." She stood, crossing her arms over her chest and walking to the window. For a long, long time she stared out the window, watching the moonlight dance along the treetops and the roof line.

Then she took a deep breath and sighed. "I don't know if my father ever had a profession other than gambling. After my mother died, he moved us into a seedy hotel room in Las Vegas and had aspirations of us being some kind of father-daughter con team. He couldn't even win at Old Maid. I don't know why he thought we'd be able to con anyone." She released a dry laugh and shook her head.

"While I was growing up, he never failed to point out I owed him because he gave me life, and I believed him. It took a long time to realize the life he gave me meant nothing. By then, I'd already married Jonas Kincaid to pay the astronomical gambling debt Dad owed him."

Randy felt stabbed in the heart. He'd once asked Scarlett if she was married and she'd told him no. Had she lied? He wouldn't panic just yet. He *couldn't* panic just yet.

Scarlett continued, "I was infatuated with Jonas. He

was older, distinguished, and intelligent. I loved his good looks and his money. He pampered me, Randy. I'd never been pampered before. I even told myself I loved him.''

"So what happened to paradise?'' Randy asked in a harsher tone than he intended.

She sighed. ''About three years ago, there were some problems with Jonas's business, which put him through a lot of stress. I ignored the problems developing between us. He wanted a baby and I, like a fool, thought it might help. When I finally became pregnant, my maternal instinct kicked in and forced me to see Jonas for the evil person he is. I couldn't raise a child around him. He was obsessed and possessive, and I could sense violence brewing within him. *He* started to tell me I owed him, too.

''I was very lucky. The first two months of pregnancy were horrible, but the morning sickness stopped after that. We'd also been living on the California estate, which was not fortified with guards and a thick, high wall like the Nevada ranch. I'd spent those two months devising an escape route and one night I left, got a quickie divorce in Reno, and have been running ever since . . . Until I came here, anyway.''

Randy came to stand behind her, his hands resting upon her shoulders. He pulled her against him, and she could feel his heart pounding between her shoulder blades. His warmth felt good. His strength felt good, but she knew it wasn't enough.

Randy felt as if he'd explode. He'd never been this angry at someone he'd never even met. He didn't know who he wanted at his disposal first—Scarlett's father or Jonas. Both were snakes, low-lifes. Both of them tried to break and control Scarlett, but she'd foiled their plans. She'd gotten away. She'd gotten a divorce.

Randy felt a lot of satisfaction over old Jonas being an ex-husband instead of a dead lover. Yes, he liked dealing with a living, breathing ex-husband, instead of the exalted memories of a grieving widow.

That one, small pleasure did nothing to diminish Scarlett's obvious open wounds. She was hurting and scared and he needed to offer her support.

"It's over now, babe," he murmured into her ear. "You're safe."

She whirled about in his arms. Her look of horror and disbelief caused him to release her as if she burned his hands.

"It's not over, Randy! It'll never be over until he finds me."

Randy stepped away from her, studying her for a long time before he yanked a pair of sweatpants off the dresser and pulled them on. He dropped onto the bed, shoved both hands through his hair, and sat elbow to knee. "What is he? A G-man? A Mafia don?"

She shook her head. "He's very rich, very powerful, and very crazy. Randy, he's ruined people for giving me a lot less help than you have. I don't want him to ruin you."

"He probably intimidated them with his money. Money doesn't rule everything, Scarlett."

"It does in this case."

What she didn't say struck him more than what she did say. There was a lot more to this than what she had told him. He intended to find out. "Scarlett, what has this man got on you? I want to hear it all."

Scarlett looked at him, her tear-bright eyes shimmering in the moon's rays. "He has a pre-nuptial agreement, Randy." Her voice was thick with tears. "If we separate for any reason, I either have to pay back the ninety-two thousand dollar gambling debt my father owed or . . . or I have to give him sole custody of any children we've had!"

As Randy absorbed the magnitude of Scarlett's words, his mind worked. He tried to separate what he was thinking from what he was feeling, so he could come up with a logical solution to their problems, but he couldn't.

He loved Scarlett and he could lose her because of a pre-nuptial agreement. No! She was a grown woman and there were ways to free her of Jonas. They'd just have to find one. But would that mean giving up Hank?

Never! Hank was a little baby; a small, defenseless child. Randy wasn't about to relinquish her to some madman just because he performed the biological function which produced her.

Randy was the one who helped her be born. He'd given her a home. He'd bathed her, diapered her, and soothed her tears. She was his and he wasn't giving her up to anyone except her mother.

He looked at Scarlett. She was coiled as tight as he'd ever seen her. The fear of losing her child ate at her, fraying her senses and twisting her nerves. He'd be damned if anyone was going to do that to the woman he loved.

Randy stood and pulled her into the circle of his arms. She fit herself against him. "Scarlett, no one is going to take Hank."

"You seem so sure."

"You seem so doubtful," he countered.

She raised her face to him and studied his eyes for a long time before she nodded. "I've seen Jonas at work. He's powerful, Randy."

Randy cupped her face in his hand and smiled, slightly. "I love you and Hank, and I won't lose you to anyone. That's some powerful stuff, too . . . Trust me."

Scarlett said nothing. She wanted to remain right there in his arms for the rest of her life. She wanted to shout out the window just how much she loved this man. She wanted . . .

She wanted Randy and Hannah safe, and no matter what Randy thought, he couldn't fight someone who had as much money as Jonas.

Randy kissed her lightly then murmured, "Come back to bed and let me show you how much I love you."

Scarlett followed Randy to the huge bed expecting him to make passionate love to her. Instead, he covered her with the thick comforter and held her in his arms. With his hands stroking her back and his words soothing her nerves, she fell asleep realizing just how much Randy really did love her.

Scarlett awoke the next morning to Randy's whispered promises of what he'd do if she just opened her eyes. She eagerly obliged and they entered a world of complete bliss, complete ecstasy.

She'd decided sometime in the night, while in the warm shelter of Randy's arms, that she would abandon her fears for the weekend. He'd be on the road again on Monday and she vowed she'd find the courage to hightail it out of Dominion while he was gone. Selfish as it might seem, she wanted some beautiful memories to take with her.

She had no idea how Randy would remember this time together, if he chose to look back upon it at all. She forced herself not to consider the betrayal he'd feel. At least she'd never have to witness any painful emotions in his eyes. She'd be long gone with the knowledge that whatever he experienced from her leaving, the consequences of her staying would have been much worse.

So, Scarlett had forty-eight hours to spend with the man she loved—yes, she loved him more than anything except Hannah—and she couldn't waste one second on tears. There'd be plenty of time to cry once she severed her ties to Randy.

By Saturday afternoon they'd spent hours making love, interrupted only by caring for Hank's every need. So, Randy decided he wanted to take Scarlett for a night out on the town.

They deposited Hank into Marie's arms, and left a cooing baby and a curious woman at the Davis' front door, then headed for Wilmington.

If Scarlett planned every second, the evening wouldn't have been more perfect. They took in an old comedy festival at a refurbished movie theatre, then crossed the street to a quaint restaurant overlooking the Cape Fear River.

All the buildings were old and had been renovated for their original use or for some new purpose. The restaurant used to be a checkpoint for the pilots bringing freighters up the river during the Civil War. Not far away was the well-known Cotton Exchange which was now filled with unique shops.

A sudden heat wave brought the temperature up to spring-like conditions so, after their seafood dinner, Randy suggested, "There's an old-fashioned plank sidewalk along the river. Would you like to go for a walk?"

"Sure."

The huge orange moon called attention to itself in the indigo sky and, as if that contrast alone were not enough, it shot a spear of shimmering light across the still, cobalt water, making this a night for lovers.

Randy draped his arm along Scarlett's shoulder and smiled down at her. "You're beautiful."

She looked up at him. "So are you." And he was. The moonlight caressed his face and danced in his pale blue eyes. His smile was sweet, but hinted of the erotic little trails his lips had blazed across her body. He truly had gone where no man had gone before—to the depths of her soul. She choked back a sob. *No! You'll cry later*.

"Scarlett, I have some time scheduled off when I get back. I'd like us to go somewhere."

Scarlett chewed the inside of her jaw and said nothing.

He continued, "I'd like to take you and Hank somewhere quiet where you and I can relax, make love until we're insane and I can talk to you . . . There are things I'd like to tell you . . . Things I've never told anyone."

Scarlett's heart beat wildly. He was suggesting paradise.

She wanted to say yes so badly. Yet, she knew she'd be agreeing to something which would never happen. What should she say? And what did he mean by things he'd never told anyone?

"Hey, folks," a tall, blond man with his arm around an equally tall, blonde woman called as they met on the walk. He pointed his thumb over his shoulder indicating the direction they'd just come. "The trail ends around that curve."

"I thought it went on for at least a few more blocks," Randy said.

"It did, but some big company bought the land and took possession of the trail."

Randy nodded. "Thanks. We'll go on anyway."

The moment they cleared the curve, they could see the end of the line. Randy wished they'd turned back with the other couple.

A huge billboard, illuminated by large spotlights, put an end to the nature walk. The sign boasted of progress in the form of steel girders and glass.

Scarlett read the sign, "The future site of another Belhaven office complex." Then she said, "What a shame to lose the land to another office building."

Randy's grip tightened on her shoulder. It wasn't painful, but it was enough to bring her gaze up to his face. His features were rough, chiseled, and tight. His jaw worked like a rusty mechanism. The muscles in his neck coiled like steel cables.

"Randy?"

He released her and turned to grip the waist-high guard rail with both hands. For a long time he looked out over the water.

She touched his arm. "Randy, what's wrong?"

"I planned to tell you, Scarlett," he said in a low, hoarse voice. "I really did. I just hadn't planned to tell you tonight. It was one of those things I've never told anyone."

The sound of his voice, the rigidity of his muscles, and the pain in his eyes scared Scarlett. She couldn't imagine what affected him so. She couldn't fathom what would hurt him like this and she was afraid she'd be unable to help. "Tell me what, Randy?"

He turned and looked over her shoulder again at the billboard. His lips compressed and anger flashed in his eyes. "Belhaven . . . That is Deborah Belhaven."

Scarlett glanced at the sign in confusion. The artist's rendition of the future building was impressive. She had no doubts this Belhaven person had no financial problems. What on earth could she have to do with Randy?

Looking back at him, Scarlett asked, "You know this woman?"

"No. I know *of* this woman." He glanced at the sign once more, then at Scarlett, and then stared at his feet. "She's my mother."

Scarlett felt him tremble beneath the hand she rested on his arm. She blinked at him, a thousand questions running across her mind.

He lifted his head and answered one of those questions. "I didn't grow up in an orphanage because my parents died, Scarlett. I was there because my mother didn't want me."

TEN

Scarlett's first reaction was to fling her arms around Randy and hold on for dear life. She wanted to absorb some of the pain he so obviously felt. Yet, he'd erected a wall between them and seemed unable to handle any more physical contact than the hand she refused to remove from his arm.

Randy steadied himself by reaching back to grip the guard rail. He closed his eyes for a brief time before he opened them and looked at her. "When I found out I was leaving the home, I wanted to know something about myself . . . *Anything* about myself . . . You just don't understand the questions you have when you know nothing about your family. Was my mother pretty? Did baldness run in my family? It was like going on a trip with no road map.

"I persuaded a clerk to get my file. When I looked inside it, I felt as if I'd been hit by a truck. My mother, Deborah Belhaven, had put me up for adoption."

"Oh, Randy," Scarlett said, her words a mere gasp.

"I've tried to understand it over the years. She was only sixteen, so I'm sure it was an accidental pregnancy. She wasn't from Texas. She was from North Carolina and only stayed with a great-aunt until I was born. In fact, it was the great-aunt who actually made all the arrangements. Deborah came back here from the hospital and I went to the orphanage . . . My guess is that she hid out in Texas to avoid a family scandal since the Belhavens were the upper-crust of this area. After I was born, Deborah returned to her rich life on the Carolina coast.''

Randy's voice had turned flat. His eyes had fixed upon a point somewhere in the dark of the night and his jaw had set. The words were hard for him to say, painful, cutting. He was withdrawing from it.

This was hard for Scarlett. Being a mother herself, she couldn't imagine what would possess a woman to turn away from her child no matter what the circumstances. She was not as prepared for motherhood as she had thought and she'd been through some terrible hardships to keep Hannah out of Jonas's clutches, but abandoning her baby never crossed her mind. Hostile feelings for the woman who tossed aside a man as wonderful as Randy blurred Scarlett's vision.

She asked, ''H-Have you ever talked to her?''

Randy looked at her suddenly as if he'd forgotten she was there. ''I tried.'' He searched her face a long time then decided to tell her the whole story. ''I tried to find the great-aunt, but she had died. For a long time I felt that if Deborah didn't want me, I wanted nothing to do with her. But when the company I worked for sent me here, I became curious. Just curious.''

His expression made him seem very young and vulnerable. ''I just wanted to meet her and to see what she was like. I didn't want anything from her. We were adults. I thought we could act like adults and put aside the pain and resentment.''

''What happened?''

Randy pushed back from the rail and took a few shaky steps away from her. With his back to Scarlett, he answered her question. ''It took me about a year to get up the courage to meet her. The Belhaven estate is on the other side of the river about a mile south of here. The butler greeted me and *allowed* me to wait in the foyer while he informed my mother I was there.

"My grandfather came instead. He didn't even give me the courtesy of inviting me any further than the foyer. He demanded to know why I was there. He wouldn't believe I just wanted to meet my family and had no ulterior motive. He told me Deborah wanted nothing to do with me. I'd caused her enough pain already. But I wasn't going to leave until I heard that from my mother."

He inhaled deeply. "I guess he could see I meant it because he told the butler to ask Deborah to come downstairs."

Randy fell silent. Scarlett waited. She knew this was painful for him, but she could also sense his need to share that pain. She'd wait until he was ready.

"She never came down," he finally said, so low Scarlett moved closer so she could hear him. "Instead, she screamed at the butler so I would be sure to hear. 'I told you I don't want to see him—ever. Throw him out and tell him not to come back,' she said. Well, he didn't have to throw me out. I left that place and I swore I'd never set foot there again."

He turned to face Scarlett. "I haven't told anyone about this, not even Marie and Preston. I wasn't ashamed of my mother not wanting me when I was a baby—she was young herself—but her turning me away when I was a grown man who wasn't a threat to her . . . nearly destroyed me."

"I know it did!" Scarlett slipped her arms around his waist and pressed her cheek to his chest. His heart beat wildly against her ear. "Your *mother* should be ashamed, Randy. You did nothing wrong."

His arms slowly folded around her and he let out a long sigh. Squeezing her tightly, he said, "Oh, Scarlett, I do love you."

Scarlett looked up at him and blinked back her tears. They were tears for him. Tears for the undeserved pain and loneliness he'd suffered as a child, and the humiliation he'd endured as a man. They were tears for herself, because she knew at this moment she couldn't cause him any more pain than he'd already endured. He was under the illusion that love could conquer all, but it couldn't. Where money was concerned, love came in as a poor second.

Randy leaned down and covered her mouth with his. His lips were warm and seeking. His tongue slipped hopefully along her lips and hesitantly entered the moist cavern she opened for him. His uncertainty was as tangible as the planks beneath their feet. He needed reassurance. He needed professions of love and forever after, and Scarlett wanted to cry because she was not the woman to give it to him.

When Randy pulled away from her, she smiled weakly and whispered, "Let's go home."

The ride back to Dominion was quiet, but not tension–filled. Randy was deep in thought, although his expression wasn't grim. Scarlett snuggled next to him and periodically checked his features to assure herself he wasn't falling into melancholy.

There was no need to pick up Hannah since they'd warned Marie they might be very late and she eagerly volunteered to keep the infant all night. They had the hours until dawn all to themselves.

Turning to Randy in the semi-darkness of the apartment, she murmured, "I had a wonderful time tonight . . . And I'm honored that you shared the truth about your mother with me."

"That's not all I want to share with you." Randy encircled her waist with one arm and pulled her against the warm hardness of his body. His hand cupped her face and he kissed her deeply, possessively. She plunged her tongue into his mouth and wrapped her arms around his neck. Her fingers twisted in the curly hair spilling over his collar.

Randy scooped her into his arms and took her to the bedroom. Reverently, he removed her clothing, easing his hands over each newly uncovered inch of her flesh. His eyes soaked in the beauty of her body. His mouth tasted the sweetness of her. And when they could stand no more separation, he pulled her under him and joined their bodies with a desperate thrust.

Later, as Randy slept, Scarlett pushed a strand of hair from his brow and whispered, "I love you, Randy Taylor."

Scarlett awoke to the rude shriek of the phone the next morning. Shoving her hair from her eyes, she watched with great pleasure as Randy, naked as the day he was born, stomped into the kitchen. She smiled at the expletives he mumbled under his breath before picking up the receiver.

She lounged in the warmth he left on the bed, certain the caller was Mr. Killigrew and Randy would soon be on the road again. The thought should have pleased her—she could leave a day earlier than expected. But it shredded her insides. Soon, very soon, she'd be leaving Randy and she wondered how she'd ever survive without him.

Scarlett wasn't sure when she first realized the caller was not Mr. Killigrew. The serious tone of Randy's voice seeped slowly into her consciousness and she became intent upon what Randy was saying.

"Damn!" he cursed. "What about Hank?"

Scarlett bolted upright and swung her feet over the side of the bed. "What about Hank?"

Scarlett wrapped the sheet around her, preparing to hike barefooted to the Davis home to check on her child. Only the reassuring shake of Randy's head and the wave of his hand kept her from doing just that. Heart slamming against her chest, she waited impatiently for him to end the call.

"We'll be right there." Randy hung up the phone and came back to the bedroom. "Get dressed."

"What's wrong?" she asked as she left the bed and searched for clothes.

He scooped up his pants from the crumpled heap on the floor and pulled them on. "It's Preston. He was on his way to the restaurant for the Sunday breakfast shift and his brakes failed. He ran off the road and hit a tree."

"Oh, God!" Scarlett's heart quit pounding and shot up into her throat. "Is he . . ."

"He's okay. Luckily, someone saw him and stopped. They called a volunteer paramedic who lives about a mile from here and got him to the hospital. Damn freak accident."

Freak accident? Scarlett gulped. "You asked about Hank?"

"That was Marie. She's on her way to the emergency room so we need to go get Hank."

"And go to the hospital."

"Yes."

Scarlett yanked a sweater over her head and followed Randy into the living room. "How could his brakes fail? Preston takes such good care of his vehicles."

Randy shrugged. "But he could have forgotten to check the brake fluid. The line could have been broken or damaged somehow."

Or someone could have cut the line. Scarlett didn't like the familiar uneasy feeling creeping over her right now.

"It's a good thing he didn't have far to go or he'd have picked up a lot of speed," Randy said. Then he inhaled deeply. "Damn, Scarlett, he could have been killed!"

Randy pulled her into his arms and she held him tightly, her mind racing. *Freak accident. Brakes failed. Could have been killed*. The scenario was so similar to the ones she'd heard from people who'd helped her in her flight across the country. And after they'd told her their bad news, they'd mentioned the word which made her blood turn to ice water—Jonas.

This time, however, the bad luck occurred *before* she left. Was this incident a warning from Jonas? Was he on his way? Or was he already here—watching, waiting?

Randy pulled away from her and grabbed their coats. "We'd better get moving."

Scarlett blinked at him, hearing his voice as if it were very far away. She nodded and followed him out the door.

Scarlett and Randy didn't make it back to the apartment until seven-thirty that night. They spent half the day in the emergency room while Preston's injuries were stitched and bandaged. Scarlett shivered at the memory of his battered face and broken arm.

On the way home, they'd stopped at the station where Preston's 4 X 4 now sat in a mangled heap. The fact that he'd escaped with so few injuries proved he was on God's good side.

They'd stuck around the Davis household that afternoon, making sure the older couple was okay. Randy cooked a huge pot of chili and, while Preston slept, they ate in silence—each one deep in thought.

Randy and Marie seemed oblivious to the fact that this could be just the beginning of trouble. Even though Randy knew all about Jonas, he hadn't mentioned there might be a connection between the accident and Scarlett's ex-husband.

But the thought hadn't left Scarlett's mind all day. She felt as guilty as if she'd taken a knife to the brake line herself.

Now that they were home, Scarlett moved to the couch. She placed her sleeping baby in the drawer, thankful that Hannah was oblivious to the day's excitement. What an enviable state of being.

Randy tossed his keys on the table, the jangle sending Scarlett's frazzled nervous system into a spasm. She jolted, then whirled around and flushed when she discovered how little it took to startle her.

"Babe, you're as jumpy as a mouse in a room full of cats." Randy crossed the room and motioned her to turn around. As he massaged her neck and shoulders, he murmured close to her ear. "You're so tense."

"I guess I'm just worried about Preston."

"Yeah, me too. But the doctor said he'd be just fine."

But what about the next time Jonas strikes? Will it be you he hits? Even Randy's agile fingers couldn't lull those thoughts from her mind. Even his warmth couldn't chase away the chill of fear rushing over her.

But if she left, what insurance did she have that Jonas wouldn't hurt Randy worse than he'd ever hurt anyone? There was no way Jonas, with all his resources, wouldn't know Randy was more than just a friend to her. He could tell. He knew her so well.

Insanely jealous and obsessed, what would prevent him from sending someone back to destroy the whole town? What could she do to prevent him? Stand up to him like Randy said? She might have to sacrifice her child for Randy or sacrifice him to keep her child. What kind of choice was that?

She'd have to make a decision . . . but in the morning. In the morning, Randy wouldn't be around and she could think more clearly.

Jonas might know her well, but she was equally familiar with his method of operation. If he *was* behind the accident, of which she had little doubt, then he'd lay low tonight. After all, he knew where she was and she couldn't slip away from him. If she did manage to do that, the baby would slow her down. He probably figured she was trapped, frightened and squirming. He liked her that way, so he'd take his time in making an appearance. Right now, he'd let her work herself into a frenzy.

Wrong. Tonight, Scarlett planned to take advantage of Jonas's tactics. Tonight, she was going to drown herself in Randy's love. Passion would take the place of panic. Tonight was hers and she was going to take all she could get.

"Randy," she said huskily. "Come to bed with me."

He stepped in front of her. A fire burned in his eyes. Bold, blatant desire. Warm, tender love. He took her hands and kissed her fingertips, then led her to the bedroom.

Scarlett stopped to collect Hannah and her drawer. "I want the two people I care about most near me tonight," she told him.

Randy accepted that explanation as the closest thing to a profession of love he'd get from her.

Silently, in the smudgy glow of the winter moon, Scarlett and Randy undressed and tumbled into bed together. She rolled him onto his back and he willingly allowed her to take the lead in their lovemaking.

Knowing this was probably the last time she'd be with Randy added a bittersweetness to their union that hadn't been there before. Their simultaneous climaxes were volatile, leaving them exhausted and breathless and clinging to each other with no words to adequately express their feelings.

Scarlett checked the time. Nine-fifty-nine. Last night had been wonderful, but, in the light of day, she could feel Jonas moving in on them. Unaware of impending doom, Randy took his time getting ready for his trip. She found herself torn between pushing him out the door and pulling him into her arms.

She wasn't certain when she made the decision that leaving really was best, but now that she had, she just wanted to get it over with. Delaying the inevitable needlessly tortured her.

Scarlett watched Randy's every movement and committed it to memory. She breathed in every scent of him. Soap . . . shampoo . . . Randy. She listened intently to every sound he made. His boot heels tapping the floor. His light whistle. His clear voice as he spoke to her.

Only Hannah's distressed wails brought Scarlett out of her reverie. She picked up the baby and bounced her in an effort to appease her. It did no good.

"She's not in a very good mood today." Scarlett glanced at Randy. "She knows you're going out of town."

Randy grinned and tossed the remainder of his coffee down the drain, then put the cup in the sink. "I guess I'd better get a move on."

Scarlett looked up at him and the moment felt surreal. Here it was—the final countdown. Could she do it? Could she act as if this separation was just for a few days instead of a lifetime? Could she make Randy believe there was nothing going on here except the farewells they'd made to each other a dozen times in the last few weeks?

She swallowed and plastered a broad smile across her face as they walked to the door. Hannah bawled and kicked now. Scarlett hugged her close. *She knows. She knows and she's trying to spill the beans.*

"You be careful out there," Scarlett told Randy. "There's no telling what you might run into."

Randy grinned. "You know, I never thought I'd enjoy having someone fuss over me, but it's kind of nice." He pulled her into his arms and gave her a kiss he thought would be enough to last her the few days he'd be gone. She reached up and pulled him back to give him a kiss she hoped would last forever.

"H—m—m. If you keep that up, I'll say to hell with the trip."

Scarlett swallowed and said hoarsely, "Well, we can't have that, can we?"

Randy kissed Hannah's cheek. The baby hiccupped and snorted, then opened her mouth to scream at the top of her lungs. "I won't be gone that long, kiddo. You keep Mom straight while I'm gone." He met Scarlett's eyes, his own smoldering with memories of the last two days' intimacies. "Oh, and help her think of a date."

"A date?" Scarlett's head tilted up in curiosity.

He nodded. "One of the things I've never discussed with anyone else is a wedding date."

Only the knowledge that Hannah might be hurt kept Scarlett's knees from buckling. She blinked. He wanted to marry her!

"Randy—"

Randy silenced her protests with his lips. He kissed her long and hard, then caressed her face as he pulled away. "Just think about it and we'll talk when I get back." He opened the door and added, "I love you, Scarlett."

Scarlett leaned against the door as Randy shut it. Her whole body trembled. She hadn't expected a marriage proposal. If only . . .

Damn if only.

Her whole life had been a series of if onlys, which seemed to have worked completely against her. If only her mother hadn't died and her father hadn't drowned his sorrows in gambling. If only Jonas hadn't owned the casino where her father ran up those gambling debts and he hadn't been in the market for a vulnerable young wife.

The list went on. Jonas's embarrassment from a bad business deal—his first in twenty-five years at the top of the corporate ladder. His subsequent obsession with wiping that one smear from his record and the onset of his impotency. His jealousy over Scarlett and her heightened fear of him.

If only she hadn't hitched a ride with that family and that carload of teenagers hadn't run them off the road. Scarlett didn't wait around to see if Jonas showed up. She'd taken off on foot in all the confusion, and that's when she crossed some fields and found herself on the same deserted highway with Randy during that freak snowstorm. If only . . .

Scarlett watched Randy drive away until he was out of

sight. Numbly, she watched for awhile longer, then she looked down at Hannah. "I'm sorry, sweetie. I have to put you down while I pack."

Hannah punched angrily at the air. She was mad and wanted everyone to know it. All her fretting had engulfed her tiny face in a deep red flush.

Scarlett allowed her to protest, wishing she could join the child in a good temper tantrum. She was angry, too—angry that life had to be this way.

The phone rang and Scarlett picked up the receiver. "Hello."

"Scarlett, this is Marie."

Scarlett's throat constricted. "Marie, is everything all right? Preston?"

"He's fine, dear. I wanted to let you know a man called here for you this morning."

Scarlett felt as if she were falling from an airplane without a parachute. "A man? What was his name?"

"I don't know. He wouldn't say. He just asked if I knew you."

Scarlett stared into space. Jonas was making his move. He had targeted the Davises and if she didn't leave—

"Scarlett? Did I make a mistake?"

"No, Marie," Scarlett said, amazed at how calm she sounded. "You didn't do anything wrong. Everything is fine . . . Just fine. Look, I have to go. Hannah's screaming at the top of her lungs and I think she's hungry."

Scarlett ran to the bedroom, frantically grabbing all her belongings and stuffing them in her two shoulder bags. Her mind raced. The car seat would have to stay here. But if she took the pickup . . .

No, she was a lot of things, but a car thief wasn't one of them. Not even in this situation. She was already throwing his love back in his face as if it meant nothing to her and running away without a good-bye. She wouldn't steal from him, too. She'd find other transportation.

In her haste, she knocked the portrait he'd drawn of

them from the dresser and stepped on it, smudging the details. The irony of that broke her resistance and she allowed herself to release a few tears. When Randy returned, he'd find an empty apartment and his opinion of her would be as imperfect as the drawing was now.

Sniffing, she rolled up the paper and shoved it into one of her shoulder bags.

Hannah's wails subtly changed pitch and something about it alerted Scarlett. She ran from the bedroom, but skidded to a halt just inside the living room. Randy stood beside the table trying to comfort the screaming baby.

Randy swung around and his worried eyes met Scarlett's. The worry faded as he stared down at the shoulder bags. His gaze came back to her flushed face. A wealth of expressions marched across the blue field of his eyes—astonishment . . . disbelief . . . pain—until finally, they were devoid of all feeling. Matte blue, the sparkle died within them like a doused campfire.

Scarlett realized the full extent of why she'd wanted to avoid this scene. She imagined hurt and hate, but to watch the light fade in the eyes of someone so vibrant and full of life was as awful as having someone die in your arms.

"I forgot my wallet," he said in a low, controlled voice. "She's burning up."

Forgetting everything else for a moment, Scarlett flung the bags aside and ran to him. Her hand covered Hannah's forehead. It scalded her skin. "Oh, God! She wasn't hot a moment ago when I put her down!"

"Obviously." Randy's eyes swept back to the discarded bags, then to Scarlett, and his gaze was as searing as Hannah's skin.

"Randy—"

"Get your coat on," he ordered.

Scarlett obeyed him in silence. She'd felt her decision was for the best. She knew now that she was only making things easier for herself by not telling Randy her plans. She owed him the truth. Nothing would have changed her mind about leaving, but at least it would have been a clean and honorable break. She would have at least left him with his pride, not a sense of betrayal.

Randy held fast to Hank as he made a call. "Mr. Killigrew, this is Randy Taylor . . . I have a problem . . . my kid's sick."

Scarlett's head jerked up in surprise and she choked back her tears.

"She's only six weeks old and she's burning up with a fever. I have to take her to the hospital. If she's okay, I could leave after that, but if not . . . Well, I guess you'll have to get someone else."

"Oh, Randy! Don't do th—"

Randy's warning gaze squelched Scarlett's protest. She fell mute by his side.

"Thank you, Mr. Killigrew. I'll keep you posted." Randy hung up the phone, grabbed a blanket and wrapped Hank in it, only releasing her to Scarlett when he had to use both hands to drive.

The hospital emergency room was nearly empty when they arrived and, after filling out the necessary forms, Scarlett, Randy, and Hank were ushered into a small, white room to wait for the doctor. Scarlett huddled in the corner while Randy leaned against the wall near the door and forced himself not to look at her.

He'd not said a word to Scarlett since they left the apartment. He couldn't. He was too angry. Too hurt. Even though the suspicion Scarlett might leave was in the back of his mind, he never believed she'd actually do it. Silly of him to think his love might be worth her sticking around.

Even if Scarlett did leave, Randy felt she at least owed him a good-bye. The image of coming home to that empty apartment with no trace of Scarlett and the baby made him physically sick. If he hadn't forgotten his wallet that was exactly what would have happened.

Randy had asked Scarlett to marry him, for crying out loud. He'd never even considered that with another woman! Well, she sure let him know her feelings. She might as well have spit in his face. He felt as low as if she had.

His mother wouldn't even offer him a hello and Scarlett wasn't going to offer him a good-bye. He sure had a great batting average with women he really cared about!

The tension in the room was crushing. Hannah's screams had reached a high C level. She was uncomfortable and hurting.

Randy made himself look at Scarlett. She stared at the floor as she rocked the baby. Though silent, Scarlett's tears matched her daughter's. She was understandably upset and probably felt helpless, but no matter how much his head told him she needed his support, his heart wouldn't let him offer it. He could separate the pain of her leaving him from his common concern for Hank. All his emotions swirled around one another, related to each other. He couldn't comfort Scarlett with one hand while wanting to strangle her with the other.

The room shrank with every minute Randy and Scarlett spent in it. It was a relief when the intern joined them.

"I want to take some blood," the intern said after checking Hannah's vital signs and asking a few preliminary questions.

"Oh Lord! What's wrong with her?!" Scarlett demanded.

"Probably nothing more than a virus."

"But it could be worse!"

"I just want to cover all the bases. Does your family have a history of any diseases I should know about?"

Scarlett shook her head.

"What about you?" The intern looked at Randy.

"I'm not her father," Randy answered in a tone that sliced through Scarlett like a razor blade.

"Oh . . . I'm sorry. I-I just assumed." The young man turned back to Scarlett, his face bright red. "What about the father's family history?"

Scarlett glanced at Randy, dreading what she was about

to say, hating to do this to him, but knowing she couldn't avoid it for her baby's sake.

"Tell him about Jonas, Scarlett," Randy prodded, knowing she was delaying precious seconds of treatment for the child.

"Jonas . . . isn't Hannah's father . . . I don't know who her father is. She was artificially inseminated from a sperm bank."

Randy wasn't sure how he survived the three hours after Scarlett dropped her latest bomb on him. It hadn't been enough for her to keep him guessing about her for weeks. It wasn't enough for her to reluctantly disclose information about Jonas to him after he almost forced it from her. Nor was it enough to try to leave him without any explanation. She had to blurt out the truth about Hank's parentage in front of that poor intern.

Well, physicians were supposed to be immune to surprises. In the emergency room, nothing should come as a shock. The poor chap sure got some on-the-job training today.

Randy hadn't been trained along those lines. His relief that Hannah only had a virus, which would run its course in twenty-four hours, couldn't erase the mental torture he'd endured. He'd been on an emotional roller coaster lately, rising on the peak of love and dropping into the valley of concern for Preston. He'd reached a new level of happiness when he'd asked Scarlett to marry him, only to plummet into the depths of heartache when he found her leaving him.

And that's where he'd stayed. It had been too much for his system—worry over Hank, damaged pride over his love being unworthy, and anger over Scarlett being unable to tell him the truth about anything. His nerves had been stripped down to microscopic threads, which were threatening to snap at any moment.

Randy sighed when he exited the only pharmacy near

Dominion to find Scarlett weeping. She'd cried ever since they realized Hank was sick, but these were uncontrollable sobs. Her shoulders bobbed and she gasped for breath.

Seeing her cry still twisted his heart.

He tossed the bag of medicine onto the seat and climbed into the pickup. "Scarlett, you're going to make yourself sick if you don't quit crying. Hannah is going to be just fine."

Hannah. Not Hank. Scarlett's head jerked up and their eyes met for a brief, turbulent moment. When neither could stand what they saw, they looked away.

He thinks I'm crying because of Hannah! Scarlett wanted to wail like her baby had a few hours ago. How could Randy miss the emotions raging inside her—the sorrow, the regret, the agony of what she'd done? She'd destroyed a wonderful part of a beautiful man. How could she ever live with that?

"Randy, I'm sor—"

He raised his hand. "Don't, Scarlett! I don't want to hear it."

"I was leaving because I didn't want to hurt you!" she blurted.

He glared at her. "Well, baby, you didn't succeed."

Tears dripped off Scarlett's chin and formed wet stains in her coat. "I'm sorry I'm not as strong as you are."

"The point is, we'd be strong together. There comes a time when you have to stand up to your fears, Scarlett."

"It's not that easy!"

"Well, you have to try it to know for sure."

She sputtered, "What do you mean by that?"

"You just want an easy out. You haven't faced anything head on. You've always slinked out the back door, run in the night, left without a good-bye. Not even a good-bye, Scarlett. Damn!" The last words tore from him, leaving his throat raw.

"I was scared, Randy," Scarlett sobbed her words. "Do you know what it's like to be scared? Really scared?

Everything is so cut and dried in your book, but it's not that way in mine. There are a thousand shades of gray and millions of shadows where demons lurk. At least somebody loved *you*. Somebody took time with you and cared about you. I never had that. Do you know what it's like to have a master, Randy?"

Randy stared at her, watching the way her jaw worked and her chin jutted out. Maybe they'd taken a step too far. Maybe she was at her snapping point.

"I've had two," she said. "My father and Jonas. I've never known what it was like to be without one. So, I'm sorry if I don't know what to do with love. Damn, I don't even think I know what it is. And I'm sorry I didn't act like you thought I should. I never claimed to be a woman who deserved you or would make you happy."

She looked away. Randy held his breath and his retaliation. Her words sizzled in his brain. He didn't want them to really register because he didn't want to be humbled by them just yet. His hurt was still too new. Unable to take the confines of the pickup much longer, Randy pulled out of the pharmacy parking lot and calculated that it'd take him a good twenty minutes to get to Dominion.

The white limousine sitting among the four-wheel drives and dusty pickups in Preston's parking lot was as conspicuous as a rose in a turnip patch.

Randy noticed the car right away.

Scarlett noticed it right away.

She clutched Hannah to her and stared in horror at the vehicle with Raleigh license plates. It was Jonas. It had to be Jonas.

Randy watched Scarlett's color fade to a chalky white and her body tremble. She finally looked at him, her eyes a glossy green. "It's Jonas, Randy." Her voice was a nervous croak.

"You don't know that."

"It is! I know it is!" Hysterical now, Scarlett gazed at

the limousine. Hours ago, she might have been able to face Jonas, but that was before her role as a mother had taken its toll on her strength. She was mentally exhausted and couldn't think beyond the fact that Jonas was here to take her child away. "Randy, let me take the truck. Please. I'll leave it anywhere you want—"

"No."

She glared at him. "Fine. I'll leave on foot."

She reached for the door handle, but he stopped her. "You're not going anywhere."

"Randy, Jonas is insane. He'll do anything. Not because I'm special, but because he's lost before and he won't let that happen again. No matter what. Don't you see? He caused Preston's accident, for Pete's sake!"

Randy's eyes narrowed. "What makes you think that?"

She sighed. "It's obvious, isn't it? Preston always takes care of his vehicles. He runs off the road and then a man calls for me—"

"A man called for you? When? Why didn't you tell me?" Even as he asked, he knew the answer—she didn't trust him enough to tell him anything.

"He called Preston's house. I didn't know about it until after you left. The point is the accident, the call, and now Jonas—can't you see?!"

Randy's jaw worked for a long time before he spoke. "Scarlett, I wish you'd talked to me about this. I could have saved you some worry. When we stopped at the station yesterday, Sid told me a faulty adjustment caused the brake pad to wear out prematurely. He blames himself because one of his employees made that alignment months ago. Before we knew about you *or* Jonas. It was a coincidence."

Her eyes widened. "A coincidence?"

"Yes, and maybe the things that have scared you might be a coincidence, too. Maybe Jonas isn't as powerful as you think. He might just be a good con man who had nothing to do with the people who helped you, but you connected their bad luck with him. Maybe his power is all in your mind.''

That thought had never occurred to her. Never. Not in the five years she'd been married to Jonas and not in the months she'd spent running from him. All in her mind? Could she afford to take a chance on believing that?

"Scarlett, you've got to end this. I'll help you end it."

"Why would you help me?"

He didn't answer right away. "I'm not doing this for you." He nodded toward Hank. "I'm doing this for her."

She sighed and asked in a small voice, "H–How? How do we fight him?"

Randy thought for a moment. "First, you have to trust me. Then you have to tell me the truth. You have to tell me anything and everything we can use against him."

"Like what?"

Randy focused on Hank. "She was artificially inseminated. Tell me about it."

Scarlett swallowed hard and kept her eyes on the bar. "About three years ago, Jonas was caught in an unethical business deal. The media got wind of it and he was in all the papers. It ruined his credibility, although what he did wasn't really illegal. He started to overcompensate for his one mistake and soon became obsessed with his image.

"All the stress made him . . . impotent. At first, I figured it was a temporary thing but it lasted months, years. He wouldn't seek help. The more he worried, the worse the problem became. He thought that people could look at him and tell.

"He decided if I became pregnant, then the world would know he was a real man and I agreed to artificial insemination, hoping it would help our marriage."

"Jonas doesn't want anyone to know about this."

"He'd die before he'd let anyone know about it, he's so embarrassed. He has the medical records under lock and key."

Randy mulled this over in his mind, then asked, "What about your pre-nuptial agreement? Do you have a copy?"

She nodded. "I insisted upon that."

"Let me see it."

The agreement was brief and surprisingly not too hard to understand. Aside from the usual "what's-yours-is-yours-what's-mine-is-mine" clauses, the only thing that concerned them was the repayment of the gambling debts or relinquish the custody of any children born from the union.

"Okay. No matter what happens, stay close to me, don't offer any information, and don't let go of Hank," Randy told her.

Scarlett eyed him. "What are we going to do?"

He opened his door. "Play poker with the devil."

ELEVEN

Jonas didn't look like a giant.

Sitting in the far corner of the bar, his back to the wall and two very large henchmen nearby, he was easy to spot. But he sure wasn't the ugly monster Scarlett had painted in Randy's mind.

Looking at the lean man in his early fifties objectively, Randy would have to admit he *was* impressive. A well-built body, neatly trimmed gray hair, and a manufactured tan, he was the kind of man who could send a lady's heart into a tailspin. The smell of money drifting from his pockets probably didn't hurt his appeal with the womenfolk either.

Randy felt Scarlett become rigid beside him and his objectivity crumbled to dust at his feet. Jonas Kincaid was perverted scum who needed to be skimmed off the face of the earth.

Randy would just settle for getting him out of Scarlett's world, and he wanted her to have a big part in that elimination. She needed the security of knowing she could control her own life.

Randy glanced about the huge room. It was late enough in the afternoon for many of the regulars to already have

195

gathered in the bar. Russell and Ted were busy with one of the arcade games. Probably poker. They loved poker. Denby Foster chatted with one of the waitresses. They'd all taken time to nod greetings to Randy and Scarlett, but no one seemed to sense something was about to happen.

Randy pressed his hand in the small of Scarlett's back and said, "Come on. Let's get this over with."

Scarlett's color had evaporated from her face. Her skin, hair, and eyes turned the same pale gold. Her gaze was fixed upon the man in the corner as if he were inside the gates of hell and she was about to be tossed through it.

"Scarlett," Randy said quietly.

She jerked slightly and blinked at him.

"I'm with you," Randy assured her. "We'll do this together. He's going to be out of your life very soon. I promise."

He sure made a lot of promises, she noted. As they crossed the room to Jonas's table, the air felt thicker than cheese soup. Scarlett noted the subtle diabolic flare in Jonas's brown eyes as he watched them. She shuddered and he smiled. He enjoyed making people—especially her—uneasy.

The two gorilla-like men flanking Jonas stood, crossing their arms over their chests. Randy eyed each of them. Then he stared at Jonas.

"Well . . ." Jonas smiled, his eyes raking over Scarlett. "My dear Scarlett. At last we meet again. But you've really let yourself go. You could use a trip to Francois' and Madame Rochet's." His eyes fell upon Hannah. "You've had the child! Splendid! A boy or a girl?"

Scarlett couldn't answer. If he held a gun at her temple she couldn't have uttered a word. Her throat felt like someone had poured glue down it. Her tongue felt nailed to the roof of her mouth. If she managed to kick-start her speaking mechanisms, she couldn't have conjured up one English word to say.

She trembled like Dorothy visiting the Great and Power-

ful Oz for the first time. Jonas was all her fears rolled
into one—the boogey man, the closet monster, and the
evil beneath the bed. That was Jonas and he was within
touching distance.

She turned to Randy, hoping he'd notice the fear that
locked her knees and stole her voice. She wanted to leave
this place more than she wanted to breathe.

Randy had to admit an eerie feeling overcame him once
he'd met Jonas's eyes. They glowed like hot metal. But
a vulnerability floated just below the surface. These were
not the eyes of Satan, but an unstable man who could be
tipped over the edge. Didn't Scarlett see that? *Couldn't*
she see that?

He looked at her. No. She was caught in old fears, the
terror of a young girl trapped in situations with no way
out. She was a woman now, with options and power. If
she didn't realize that, she'd never be free of Jonas.

"It's a girl," Randy finally said, meeting Jonas's gaze
headlong.

Jonas studied him a moment, then frowned and sighed.
"Well, perhaps the second one will be a boy."

Scarlett's head jerked up, horror blazed in her eyes.

"Well, now that this is over," Jonas said as he stood.
"Come along, my dear, and let's go home."

Scarlett bolted like a filly facing her first saddle. Randy
pulled her into his steadying arms and informed Jonas,
"She's not going anywhere with you."

The older man raked an annoyed glance over Randy,
then directed his words to Scarlett, "My dear, haven't you
told him what I can do?"

Scarlett said quietly, "I told him."

"So, your little friend here thinks he's a big man."
Jonas gave him the once over again and smiled. "He
wouldn't even work up a good sweat for my men. Scarlett,
go to the car and let me take you and our child home."

Scarlett instinctively hugged Hannah closer to her.

"She is home." Randy stood his ground.

There was a brief delay before Jonas laughed. "With you? You can't afford her. You can't afford to take her from *me*."

"Which brings us to the pre-nuptial agreement," Randy said.

"You are out of your league, cowboy. Like I said before, you can't afford to take her from me." He looked at Scarlett. "Don't worry, my pet. I have no intention of taking the child from you. I plan to take you both."

"Not if she repays the gambling debt," Randy interjected.

Jonas snorted. "I know she doesn't have it and *you* look as though you have even less. Good grief, my dear, you *have* scraped the bottom of the barrel, haven't you?"

Scarlett's head lifted as she felt a surge of courage. "Randy is a good man, Jonas! He's been good to me! He's not the bottom of the barrel. He's the best thing that has ever come into my life!"

Stunned, Randy eyed her. His heart pounded rapidly against his chest. What she'd admitted was small, but it was a start toward a future—yes, he still would like a future with her.

The fact that she'd stood up to Jonas hadn't slipped by Randy either. All she had to do was keep it up and they'd be home free, judging from the slight crimson tinge of her ex-husband's face.

Jonas shrugged as if mildly inconvenienced, but his voice was laced with much more. "I seem to have underestimated you, sir. I thought you'd be as harmless as a gnat. It seems I have a swarm of hornets on my hands."

Jonas's nod was slight, but Randy saw it and prepared himself for the goon who lunged at him from the right. A good side-kick to the man's groin sent him sprawling to the floor, curling in pain as he covered his injury with trembling hands.

Randy stepped out of the second man's path, sending him plowing into Russell's abundant belly.

As his friend repaid the henchman for interrupting his video game, Randy faced Jonas.

Kincaid regarded his men with disgust then lifted his evil eyes. "You can kill those men and I'd get more to find her. I have the agreement and the law on my side!"

Something about Jonas's voice pulled Scarlett's attention from the men on the floor to him. There was a childish whining twang in his tone. She'd never heard that before. Could Jonas's hold on sanity be slipping? No.

Randy had made no reply; his mind was occupied with his plan of action. He knew one thing for sure—there was no way in hell he'd let Jonas leave with a legal leg to stand on. Scanning the gathering crowd, Randy spotted the wide-eyed little man hiding among some long-legged waitresses. "Denby."

"Y–Yes?" Denby took a timid step forward.

"Do you still want my truck?"

"No, Randy!" Scarlett protested. "Don't do this because of me!"

"Hush, Scarlett!" Randy gave her a warning glare then looked back at Denby. "Do you still want the truck, Denby?"

"I sure do."

"Then write this man a check for ninety-two thousand dollars and it's yours."

"I'm not taking a check from that little degenerate!" Jonas interjected. "He looks like a street person!"

Randy suddenly took a step toward Jonas. He reached out and twisted the man's thousand dollar suit lapels in his hands, pinning him against the wall. "Now, you listen to me! I've already had enough of you. Scarlett's had everything *she's* going to take from you. Now, you're going to take the check, leave here, and never bother Scarlett again. Do you hear me?!"

Jonas grinned. His expression became weird, wild. "Why should I? The baby is mine and the woman is mine. I *own* her."

Randy growled, "The woman doesn't belong to you! And is the baby really yours, my man?"

"W—What?" Jonas's voice trembled.

Randy lowered his voice. "She doesn't look like you . . . In fact, she looks like me. What if I told you I was in California about ten and a half months ago?"

Randy's words produced the desired effect. Jonas gulped for air. His right eye twitched and he trembled with fear or rage. It made no difference which one. Either would help deteriorate the rational demeanor he tried so hard to present.

"You—you aren't her father," Jonas stammered.

"You don't seem too sure of that. Why? Think I might be telling the truth?" Randy tilted his head. "Why don't we just go to court to prove the kid's paternity?"

Scarlett watched Jonas in amazement. Sweat rolled into his eyes and beaded on his upper lip. He stared at Randy with panic and glanced at her with apprehension. He twitched and fidgeted, contrary to his usual confident, poised self.

Could Randy be right? Jonas was just a man? A con man who specialized in using other people's hardships to his advantage? Was the demigod dissolving before her eyes?

Scarlett was legally bound to repay her father's gambling debt or release custody of her child. If Randy took care of the money, Jonas had no right to claim Hannah. Even if he tried, a few tests could prove he wasn't her father.

However, Jonas was mentally unstable and might try to cause trouble, possibly even threaten lives. But she could divulge embarrassing facts about his personal life, couldn't she? Yes. His believing she'd announce his "inefficiencies" to the public was the only insurance she needed to keep Jonas at bay.

A fog lifted from Scarlett as she saw things clearly for the first time in her life. She looked down at her baby and then at Randy. She had a chance to be happy, to control her own life. She had leverage and power that she never knew she possessed and if she didn't take some action, she'd be running all her life. She'd lose everything that mattered to her.

She looked at Jonas. The great wizard had been discredited.

Scarlett took a courageous step forward. "It's over, Jonas."

"Wh–What?!" Jonas's eyes weren't evil now. They were astonished and apprehensive.

"It's over. Give it up. You're getting your money and that's all you're going to get. I'm not running from you anymore. If you want to try to take my baby or cause the people I care about any trouble, you go right ahead. But I've got a lot of things I'd like to get out in the open about you."

Jonas wasn't going down easily, "Nothing you say will be believed."

For a moment, her newborn strength faltered. He was probably right. She swallowed and forced herself to be brave. Everything counted on her next words. "Maybe not, but do you want to take that chance? The media would have a ball with what I'd tell them and by the time you proved it false, it would already be in the public's mind. You'd be linked with abuse, obsessive behavior, impo—"

"Shut up! Shut up!" Jonas cried out.

Randy took over. "You have one of two options. You can take the money, release Scarlett from the contract, and leave us alone forever. Or you can be stubborn and risk all your secrets being tomorrow's news." Then Randy bluffed him. "And don't even think about trying to eliminate us because we've got information stashed away in several places which will be released should anything happen to us."

Jonas's eyes rounded.

"So, my man, what will it be?" Randy prodded.

Kincaid stared at Randy, then his gaze darted to Scarlett.

She could see the fight fade from his eyes. As long as he had her shaking in her shoes at the sight of him, he had a chance. When she stood up to him, he'd crumbled like a playground bully receiving some of his own medicine.

Jonas slumped defeatedly. "What do you want me to sign?"

Moments later, Scarlett watched in stunned silence as Jonas marked the pre-nuptial agreement paid-in-full and signed it. He scribbled his signature on another paper stating he and Scarlett had no further business and he agreed to stay out of her life. Nora, one of the regulars at the bar, notarized the papers.

Jonas's brown glare raked over Scarlett and her insides quivered. He snarled, "I wouldn't want you now, anyway. Not after that lowlife ruined you."

She lifted her chin. "He didn't ruin me, Jonas. He washed away your scum."

Jonas's jaw worked as he bit back his reply. He called to his deflated warriors and they hurried from the bar.

Silence fell upon the room as everyone watched him go. Most were not certain what had just happened, but they could see the weight literally lift from Scarlett's shoulders.

"Did we do a good thing?" Russell asked Randy.

He smiled. "We did a good thing, Russ."

Russell nodded. "Good. Let's drink to it, then."

As his friend ambled to the bar and received a free beer, Randy looked around for Scarlett. She'd dropped onto a nearby chair, clutching Hank to her like a lifeline. Her eyes glittered with unshed tears. Exhaustion hung onto her features like heavy rocks.

She smiled weakly at him. "You were right. All that time I ran from him, he terrorized me, controlled me, and it would have been over if I just stood up to my fears.'' She gazed at the floor. ''It's over. It's really over.''

He suddenly felt awkward. An unexplainable dread overcame him. ''It's over,'' he said quietly. ''What you did took a lot courage. I'm proud of you.'' When she looked up, he extended the notarized papers to her. ''Here. You're free.''

Free. Scarlett's words came back to play in his mind like a scratchy record. *I don't know what love is . . . Have you ever had a master? . . . No one's ever been kind to me without asking for something in return. . . .*

Her words pounded in his head with each beat of his heart. He'd just paid a debt for her . . . Now did she expect him to hand her a bill? If he asked for her love, would he be no better than Jonas and her father? He wanted her to feel love, not obligation.

It didn't matter what his reasons for wanting her to care about him were, he asked for the same thing all the other men in her life demanded. How could she know the difference?

Scarlett took the papers and Randy shoved his shaking hands into his pockets. His chest constricted around his heart and his throat thickened until he couldn't even swallow. He loved Scarlett, but she'd never been allowed the freedom to choose who *she* wanted.

To Scarlett, love was an IOU.

Well, no more. Randy helped her gain her freedom from Jonas and he was going to go the whole way. He was going to free her from the vicious merry-go-round she'd been trapped on all her life.

''Well,'' he said, surprised his voice even worked at all. ''I think I'll be going.''

He turned and took a few steps before her hand pressed between his shoulder blades. Her voice was low and husky when she asked, ''Where? Where are you going?''

''For a ride,'' he answered. He thought he could tighten

his muscles and never feel her. But he did. Her touch burned clear through to his heart.

"Then I'll go with you."

Randy steeled himself and swung around to face her. The sight of her shattered his heart into a million pieces. This was crazy. She was the woman he loved and he should take her under any terms he could get her. Who cared if she felt obligated to him?

He cared. It might be good between them for awhile, but what would happen when she realized he fell into the same category as Jonas? She only thought she loved him when it was really obligation she felt. He'd rather have his heart shredded now.

"No, you can't go with me," he said at last.

"No? But we have to talk," Scarlett insisted.

"There's nothing to talk about."

"I think there's a lot to talk about. If you're still angry with me about leaving, then let's argue it out! Don't walk away."

A moment of crackling silence fell between them as they both recalled *she* was the one walking away only a few hours ago.

"It has nothing to do with your leaving," Randy said. "Now, I understand why you did."

"Then . . . what?"

Randy closed his eyes. He understood *too* much now.

"I love you!" Scarlett said desperately.

Randy'd longed to hear those words and now they held no meaning for him. How many times had she said it to Jonas? He looked at her. "Oh, babe," he croaked, "how do you know?"

Scarlett's eyes widened. "What do you mean? I know when I love someone."

"Like you loved Jonas? Your father? You said it yourself this afternoon. You aren't even sure you know what love is."

Her mouth opened then closed again.

Randy sighed. "See? You've given exactly what you thought everyone wanted. You gave what you thought was love. But you don't even know what it is. When it's demanded, it's not love."

"But you're different!" she cried.

"How? I did something big for you and now you feel obligated. You know it will make me happy to hear you say you love me . . . I won't have you trade one master for another."

"Randy," she said in a breathless whisper. "Why are you doing this?"

He looked from her to the baby nestled in the crook of her arm and back again. "Because for the first time in my life, I love someone enough to give her exactly what she needs even if it isn't me."

Randy leaned down with the intention of giving Scarlett a soft farewell kiss, but she curled her hand behind the back of his neck and pulled him to her. A primal cry left her throat as her mouth covered his. Lips, tongues, and souls melted into one another. Hands clung in desperation. Randy was lost in the taste, the feel, the smell of her. He was just plain lost.

Then reality elbowed its way into Randy's head and he pried himself away from Scarlett. He stared down at her face. The simple beauty of it took his breath away. Would he ever forget the exact placement of every freckle scattered upon her milky skin? Would he ever forget the green fire of her eyes? Would the golden color of her hair ever slip from his memory? He doubted it.

He wanted to smile for her, but couldn't. He spoke in a coarse murmur. "Have a good life, babe . . . Goodbye."

Not wanting anyone to see him lose control, he plowed through a gathering of Preston's patrons on the way to the door.

Scarlett shouted, "You're wrong, Randy Taylor! One day, I'll make you see it!"

Just before the door closed behind Randy, he heard Hank's bone-crumbling cries.

"Star."

Silence.

"Lone Star."

Randy glared at the CB, pulled away from the pickup door, and tried to work out the kinks in his back. He shifted his long legs on the seat, the movement sending a crushed beer can to join a half dozen others on the floor.

"Dammit, Randy! I know you're out there! Answer me!"

Dixie's use of his real name caught his attention. He wasn't aware she knew anything but Lone Star. He grabbed the CB from its slot. "I'm here."

"Well, thank you!" Dixie said, exasperation and agitation swirling in her tone. "How long have you been listening to me?"

He didn't answer.

She didn't care. "You have scared everyone half to death! Where are you?!"

"In a safe place," he responded, not ready to tell her just yet.

He scanned the area. After leaving Preston's three days ago, he'd stopped for provisions then headed for the sanctity of the hunting lodge. This time of year, it was deserted and offered the best place to breed the kind of self-pity he desired. With no telephone, no television, and only a radio which furnished sad country songs, he'd elevated feeling sorry for himself to an art form.

He hadn't started drinking until last night, though. The last thing he really remembered was popping the top of his umpteenth beer and sitting beside the wood stove. He had no idea when he'd gone back to the truck and downed another six pack. Now he could add a monstrous hangover to his miseries.

"Everyone was afraid you'd done something drastic, but I told them you're not that stupid . . . Are you?"

Randy smiled wryly. "Thanks for the vote of confidence, Dix." He ran a hand along his chin, scraping a considerable growth of beard. A yank of the rearview mirror in his direction displayed a frightening sight.

Never one to be overly concerned about his looks, Randy *had* always been a hygiene nut. He'd sure abandoned that habit over the last three days. He couldn't remember ever looking worse.

Red lines shimmied across the whites of his eyes. Dark smudges of fatigue hung beneath his lower lids and drooped into the stubble shadowing his cheeks. His hair must have grown two inches! Shaving his head and starting over was a better alternative than attempting to plow a comb through the tangled mass.

Randy's senses kicked in. He sniffed. *Stale beer. Onions? Yeah, but what's that other odor? Have mercy! Me!* Well, technically it was his clothes. Ripe!

Randy rolled down the window and took in long swigs of cool winter air. *Ah, redemption!*

"Randy, Scarlett told m—"

"Scarlett?!"

"Yeah, she reached me on the CB. She wanted me to try to locate you. Where are you?"

Damn! He figured Scarlett had probably left town by now. He'd been gone long enough. "I'm okay."

"Yeah." Dixie didn't sound convinced. "Well, she told me what happened. I'm sorry."

Leaning back inside, Randy eyed the radio and ran a hand through his hair. His fingers snagged in a tangle and he had to work his hand free. "Me, too. She's never been able to feel an honest emotion in her life. I had to give her a chance."

"You were very noble."

"Yeah . . . Well, love stinks, Dix." *And so do I.*

She laughed. "Don't I know it!"

Silence fell between them, then he said truthfully. "I didn't mean to scare anyone. I just couldn't face that apartment."

"Too many memories?"

"Yeah."

"Hey, I have an idea! Why don't we meet somewhere for a drink and I'll tell you about *my* pitiful love life. It ought to be sad enough to keep your mind off your own."

Randy perked up. The drink didn't appeal to him. The prospect of meeting his friend after all this time did. He also would welcome anything to take his mind off Scarlett and Hank, even for a second.

"Sure, but I need to get cleaned up a bit first. Believe me, in my present state, I could rid the territory of all its vegetation just by walking by it."

Two hours later, Randy had taken a shower and changed into some clean clothes. His spirits weren't high by the time he reached the outskirts of Wilmington, but the anticipation of meeting Dixie kept his mind off the empty ache which had been his companion for the last few days.

He turned into the parking lot of Dapper's, a well-known Wilmington bar, for his rendezvous with Dixie. Stopping the pickup just inside the entrance, he looked for her rig and his heart shot into his throat.

The only semi intimidating the smaller vehicles occupying the area was not the gold-and-black Kenworth Dixie described as hers. This rig was blue and chrome. A Peterbilt.

A car horn blasting behind Randy jolted him into moving his pickup into the lot. He inched toward the ten-wheeler, staring at it a long time before he got out to see if what he suspected was true.

The cold air frosted his breath as he walked to the semi's door and pressed his hand on the silver star he knew he'd find. *His* truck. What was going on? Why was his truck here? And where the hell was Dixie?

He closed his eyes and shook his head, vaguely aware of a car driving by. Only the sound of spewing gravel as the car skidded to a halt pulled Randy from his confused thoughts.

He recognized that car—Marie's station wagon. He also recognized the woman who slammed the driver's door and marched toward him.

Scarlett.

As he watched her approach him, his pulse raced and his throat became so dry he couldn't swallow. The bright street lights overhead ignited a green fire in her eyes. She was angry, but even furious she was the most beautiful thing he'd ever seen. Had it only been three days since he left her at Preston's?

"Scarlett—"

"I ought to belt you!" Scarlett shouted.

"Why?"

"Leaving like that!" She took a step forward, maneuvering him toward the right.

"Scarlett—"

"Scaring all of us! Disappearing for three days!" She advanced and he retreated.

"I wish one woman on this earth would let me finish a sentence! Now, Scarlett—"

"Not practicing what you preach!" She moved closer.

He took a step backwards and collided with his truck. "What?"

" 'There comes a point when you have to stand up to your fears, Scarlett'," she repeated his own words to him and he winced. "And you think *I'm* the one who hasn't felt an honest emotion?!"

Scarlett twirled around and headed for the station wagon. Her words registered and he stalked her. "Hey! You listened to my conversation with Dixie!"

Scarlett tossed him an irritated glance.

"Scarlett, what's going on? How did my truck get here?"

"Russell and Ted brought it over."

"What? How did—" Randy stopped talking and walking when he caught sight of the three people piling out of the station wagon. Marie and Preston . . . And a woman at least ten years older than Dixie claimed to be.

She was an elegant woman despite her casual clothes. Randy got the feeling those casual clothes probably cost more than his entire winter wardrobe. He bet the gold adorning her neck and wrists was real, too.

She took a few tentative steps around to his side of the car and he could see she was tall and thin. Warm chestnut and pale gray colored her short curls and her eyes were a clear, pale blue.

Those eyes watched him in a way that caused a current of dread to skip over his insides. "Scarlett, that's not Dixie, is it," he stated more than asked.

Scarlett's expression softened and she shook her head. "No. Dixie's on her way to Georgia. I contacted her over the CB and asked her to help me arrange this. I felt the prospect of meeting Dixie after all this time might appeal to you so much you wouldn't suspect anything."

"What should I have suspected?" He wasn't sure he wanted to know.

Scarlett hesitated for a long time before she looped her arm through his and motioned toward the woman with the brown curls. "Randy . . . this is Deborah Belhaven."

Randy's eyes darted from Scarlett to Marie and Preston, then came to rest on Deborah Belhaven. He yanked himself free of Scarlett's hold and moved away. His chest felt as if it would explode. His ears rang and his eyes blurred. Rage. Humiliation. Betrayal. A thousand emotions pulverized him all at once and he sought the support of the car hood because he didn't think his knees could support the burden of it all.

He hauled air into his lungs and focused upon a decorative ridge in the hood in an effort to gain control again.

Scarlett moved to his side and tried to slip her arms

around his waist, but he twisted away. She stared at him, horror and tears filling her eyes.

Randy leaned his back against the car door and ground out, "Are . . . all of you . . . sadistic?"

Scarlett took a step toward him, but he stopped her with one enraged glare. She jerked as if she'd been slapped.

"You," Randy growled at her. "I told you about *her* because I trusted you! You told everyone and then you talked her into meeting me! You used Dixie? Russell? Ted? Damn, Scarlett, you knew what that would do to me!"

"Randy," Scarlett's voice trembled with desperation. "I didn't do this to hurt you."

He managed to release a wry laugh. "Well, you missed your mark, my dear." He glared at the Davises. "The joke's over."

Marie was pale. Preston was frowning.

"This is no joke," Scarlett said in a small voice.

Randy's eyes flickered in white-hot flames as he stared at her. He visibly trembled with insurmountable rage and unbearable pain. "Well, whatever it is, I don't need it."

He pivoted and headed away from the four people who'd stripped him of everything. They'd betrayed him, humiliated him. Well, he had no ties anywhere now. He had no truck and no job. His friends had turned against him and the woman he loved crushed him. He could leave all his heartaches right here in North Carolina. Maybe he'd move to Canada for awhile.

"They told me you were dead!" Deborah shouted.

Randy stopped in his tracks, but didn't turn around.

"I was sixteen. Your father was twenty-four and in the Navy. His name was Daniel Monroe and I loved him more than I loved life itself."

Randy faced her. He expected to find lies in her eyes. He was so tired of lies and secrets! But Deborah's eyes were those of a drowning person who had to convince someone to throw her a life preserver.

Deborah stepped closer, but not too close. She looked at Randy, meeting his eyes, facing his judgment. "Your father was a good man. He was kind and gentle. His only crime was not being born rich. My father restricted us from seeing each other, but it didn't stop us.

"Daniel had six months left on his tour of duty when he shipped out. His ship had gone down at sea by the time I found out I was pregnant . . . My father wanted me to have an abortion, but I told him I'd tell the entire country I was pregnant if he made me. He'd do anything to avoid a scandal, so he sent me to stay with my aunt in Texas until you were born. I was planning to run away with you."

Deborah sighed and wiped away a new tear inching down her cheek. "I had a rough delivery and they knocked me out. When I awoke . . . When I awoke, they said I'd struggled too long. The umbilical cord was wrapped about your neck and you had died." She cried her last words. After a moment, she straightened her back and continued. "I was devastated. I'd lost everyone . . . Daniel . . . my baby."

Randy looked at Scarlett who cried the tears he couldn't shed. He was beyond tears. He was beyond rage and hate. He was numb.

"Until Scarlett came to see me two days ago, I had no idea you even existed."

Scarlett explained, "I went to ask her if she would help me get your truck back. I figured she owed you that much. She almost had a heart attack when I told her about you."

Randy still didn't buy it. He faced the woman with eyes he refused to admit looked too much like his own. "If *she* bought the truck from Denby, then I don't want it."

"Randy," Deborah appealed, "don't do something you'll regret."

"The only thing I regret is this unbelievable scene!" He started to walk away, then asked, "If you were so devastated then why did you send me away?"

"I told you they knocked me out and—"

"Not when I was born!" Randy shouted, his voice thundering across the parking lot. "When I went to your home a few years ago."

Deborah took a weary breath. "Randy, I didn't know you ever came to my home until Scarlett told me. I didn't send you away."

"I heard you tell the butler to have me thrown out," he snapped. "You can't deny what I heard with my own ears."

Deborah's lips compressed then she stated quietly, "I don't doubt you heard *someone*, but did you ever see *me*?"

Randy blinked at her, then looked at Scarlett. "I don't know why you're doing this, but it's not going to work. Even if I wanted to believe this story, I wouldn't because I don't trust you."

Scarlett choked on her tears and shook her head. This was backfiring on her. She'd hoped for a happy reunion between mother and son. Now Randy thought everyone he cared about had ganged up on him in a horrible joke. Scarlett realized too late how heartless this plan of hers was. Of *course* he had every right to be upset and suspicious when she sprang it on him like this. She should have thought before she took action.

"Randy," Deborah said, "I don't know what happened when you came to my house, but please don't be angry at Scarlett for this. She only wanted to help."

When he didn't respond, Deborah sighed and continued. "My father was responsible for our being separated when you were born, so he'd do anything to keep me from finding out you were alive. I was traveling a lot a few years ago and I suspect you came to the estate then. Father could have ordered a maid or the cook to say whatever you heard. I don't know. He's dead or I'd make him account for what he did."

Randy stared at the ground. He'd never actually seen

Deborah, only heard a woman's voice. What she said made sense, but he just couldn't believe it. Old hurts wouldn't let him.

Deborah reached out to touch him, then thought better of it and retracted her hand. "I know you suffered, but so did I. I missed out on all those years!

"Well, I've done what I came here to do," Deborah said when he made no response. She stiffened her back and looked at Scarlett. "Would you mind taking me home?"

"Not at all," Scarlett said, her eyes fixed on Randy.

Deborah gazed longingly at him. "Good-bye, Randy."

His eyes darted up, catching Scarlett's anxious stare, then he switched to Deborah's retreating figure. He watched her for a long time, swallowing over and over. One word kept repeating itself in his mind. It was a word he'd whispered in his bed at night as a child and a word he'd only thought of as an adult. One word and it was so hard to say when someone could hear. But he had to try. He opened his mouth and spoke the one word he'd never had the privilege to use before. "Mother?"

Deborah whirled around and blinked disbelievingly at him. He eyed her, wondering what to do next. She solved his problem by running to him and pulling him into her arms. "Oh, son!" she cried, kissing his cheek.

Randy wasn't sure how much time passed before he searched for Scarlett. She stood nearby, her eyes full of hope and tears. He smiled and held out his hand to her. She eagerly entwined their fingers, then slipped her arms about him and his mother.

"Woman, you are something else!" Randy said a few hours later as he and Scarlett snuggled among the tangled sheets of a motel bed. After all the apologies and tears, the Davises took Hank and Deborah back to Dominion to prepare for a celebration party.

Randy had taken Scarlett to the first motel they'd seen and they'd immediately fallen into bed.

"If I live to be a hundred, you will never cease to surprise me!" he exclaimed.

"That's what keeps you interested."

He tipped up her chin to kiss her, his tongue seeking the moist recesses of her mouth just as his body had sought her body only moments before.

As they pulled from the kiss, Scarlett asked, "Are we even now? Debts paid? Equal ground?"

"Hm. I don't know . . . I might owe you some."

Scarlett groaned. "If I live to be a hundred, you will never cease to aggravate the hell out of me!"

He laughed and rolled over onto his back, pulling her with him. The movement settled her on him so they were joined. She gasped and leaned forward, sheathing them in the curtain of her silky hair. Her head lolled against his. "Or send my hormones over the edge."

"It keeps you interested."

Scarlett straightened and splayed her hands on his chest to massage it as she moved back and forth and side to side.

He groaned and cupped her smooth buttocks in his hands.

Scarlett looked down at him. "Are we on equal ground?"

"Oh, yes!"

"And you aren't mad at Dixie?"

"I'm not mad at *anyone* right now."

A smile lifted the corners of her mouth as she ran a hand along his cheek. "I never, ever meant to hurt you. No one did. We were only trying to do what we thought was best for you."

"I know." A serious expression invaded his features. "I think you and I learned a lot about love, commitment, and trust."

"Yes." She nodded. "I love you, Randy Taylor."

"I love you, too."

Scarlett arched her back, pressing her hands on his thighs for support. As she rocked on him, his arousal stiffened and filled her. His hands slid around her hips and up the ripples of her rib cage until he supported a creamy, pink-tipped mound of flesh in each of his hands. She whimpered as he worked his thumb against each pebble-hard nipple.

"Dixie was right," he commented.

Scarlett opened her eyes a little and looked at him. "About what?"

"I *do* have Scarlett fever."

He rolled over so that she was beneath him and as he covered her mouth with his kisses and filled her body with his, he realized happily that his was an incurable fever.

EPILOGUE

"Make the new car go faster, Daddy!"

Randy tried to focus on three-and-a-half-year old Hank's face in his rearview mirror, but since she was strapped into the car seat, he got a view of chestnut curls instead. He groaned and ventured a glance to his right. Scarlett, arms crossed, regarded him with a perturbed expression.

His shoulders raised, then lowered, and he gave her a weak smile. "She likes to go fast."

"I knew you took her for joyrides!" Scarlett exclaimed. "Honestly, she gets more like you everyday."

Randy couldn't help but grin at his wife's statement. It amazed him just how much alike he and Hank were. Aside from the physical similarities, their personalities matched point for point. Happy-go-lucky, friendly, easygoing.

"Honey, I don't think we should go too fast in Mommy's condition," Randy spoke over his shoulder.

"Aw—w—w!" Hank commented and leaned back against her seat in disappointment.

Randy patted Scarlett's rotund stomach and smiled. "How we doing there?"

"I'm fine. The baby is doing cartwheels."

"I told you he wouldn't like that stuff Mom calls barbecue. The boy wants Texas-style food!"

"You're going to insist it's a boy until the end, aren't you?" Scarlett smiled at him.

God, he loved her smile. He loved his life. He said seriously, "I do it just to goad you. I'd really prefer another girl so I can be surrounded by beautiful women."

She laughed. "You're a silver-tongued devil."

The last word brought another devil to mind. Jonas. So much had happened since they'd run him out of Preston's that February afternoon nearly four years ago.

He couldn't believe how much had changed, how many *good* things had happened to him. He and Scarlett had wasted no time getting married. They were married at Preston's with all the regular customers as guests. Deborah was there and cried through the whole ceremony.

She wasn't that sentimental in business, however. The tough cookie brought Randy into her business at the bottom. Well, near bottom, anyway. He'd worked his way up through the ranks to director of operations and it'd been damned hard work, too.

His mother had plans for him to be CEO one day, but she wanted him to know the company inside and out. It didn't hurt for the employees to know their future boss had once worked beside them on the loading docks, either.

Randy built a small home for his family halfway between Preston's house and Deborah's estate. He was now adding a little darkroom for Scarlett since she'd discovered a talent for photography. Little by little, they were acquiring the things they dreamed of having.

Three months after Randy and Scarlett became husband and wife, they received word that Jonas had committed suicide. Randy didn't feel happy over the death, but he couldn't deny he felt relief. As long as Jonas lived, it was in the back of Randy's mind that he could always cause trouble.

Randy had already begun adoption proceedings for Hank before Jonas died. The news assured Randy that nothing stood in the way of making that child his. No man on earth could have loved her any better. She was as much his child as the one Scarlett carried right now. He recognized it, his loved ones recognized it, and now the law did, too.

Randy had a good life and he owed it all either directly or indirectly to the woman sitting on the passenger side of his brand new Mercedes. He turned to her and said, "I love you."

She smiled at him. "I love you, too."

Randy settled back in the plush seat to enjoy the ride home after his mother's annual Fourth of July cookout.

"Uh–oh."

"Uh–oh? What's uh–oh?" He felt a sickening sense of *déjà-vu* as he met Scarlett's weak smile.

"Ah . . . My water broke."

Hank called from the back seat. "What water?"

"Nothing," Randy told her then gaped at the wet spot on the red velour seat and groaned. "My new car seat, Scarlett!"

"*Our* car seat, dear," Scarlett smiled with honest amusement.

Randy checked for traffic then made a U-turn for Wilmington. "I can't believe this! Twice in a lifetime! You're making a habit of this! Well, at least it's not snowing this time."

Scarlett was determined not to argue. "Look at it this way. At least you're experienced."

Randy's brow shot up, then he laughed. "I'm not delivering *this* baby, Scarlett. One is enough."

Scarlett gave him a wickedly teasing smile.

"I'm not," Randy repeated.

And he kept repeating it as he drove into the worst Fourth of July traffic jam to hit Wilmington in fifteen years.

SHARE THE FUN . . .
SHARE YOUR NEW-FOUND TREASURE!!

You don't want to let your new books out of your sight? That's okay. Your friends can get their own. Order below.

No. 47 STERLING'S REASONS by Joey Light
Joe is running from his conscience; Sterling helps him find peace.

No. 48 SNOW SOUNDS by Heather Williams
In the quiet of the mountain, Tanner and Melaine find each other again.

No. 49 SUNLIGHT ON SHADOWS by Lacey Dancer
Matt and Miranda bring out the sunlight in each other's lives.

No. 50 RENEGADE TEXAN by Becky Barker
Rane lives only for himself—that is, until he meets Tamara.

No. 51 RISKY BUSINESS by Jane Kidwell
Blair goes undercover but finds more than she bargained for with Logan.

No. 52 CAROLINA COMPROMISE by Nancy Knight
Richard falls for Dee and the glorious Old South. Can he have both?

No. 53 GOLDEN GAMBLE by Patrice Lindsey
The stakes are high! Who has the winning hand—Jessie or Bart?

No. 54 DAYDREAMS by Marina Palmieri
Kathy's life is far from a fairy tale. Is Jake her Prince Charming?

No. 55 A FOREVER MAN by Sally Falcon
Max is trouble and Sandi wants no part of him. She *must* resist!

No. 56 A QUESTION OF VIRTUE by Carolyn Davidson
Neither Sara nor Cal can ignore their almost magical attraction.

No. 57 BACK IN HIS ARMS by Becky Barker
Fate takes over when Tara shows up on Rand's doorstep again.

No. 58 SWEET SEDUCTION by Allie Jordan
Libby wages war on Will—she'll win his love yet!

No. 59 13 DAYS OF LUCK by Lacey Dancer
Author Pippa Weldon finds her real-life hero in Joshua Luck.

No. 60 SARA'S ANGEL by Sharon Sala
Sara *must* get to Hawk. He's the only one who can help.

No. 61 HOME FIELD ADVANTAGE by Janice Bartlett
Marian shows John there is more to life than just professional sports.

No. 62 FOR SERVICES RENDERED by Ann Patrick
Nick's life is in perfect order until he meets Claire!

No. 63 WHERE THERE'S A WILL by Leanne Banks
Chelsea goes toe-to-toe with her new, unhappy business partner.

No. 64 YESTERDAY'S FANTASY by Pamela Macaluso
Melissa always had a crush on Morgan. Maybe dreams do come true!

No. 65 TO CATCH A LORELEI by Phyllis Houseman
Lorelei sets a trap for Daniel but gets caught in it herself.

No. 66 BACK OF BEYOND by Shirley Faye
Dani and Jesse are forced to face their true feelings for each other.

No. 67 CRYSTAL CLEAR by Cay David
Max could be the end of all Crystal's dreams . . . or just the beginning!

No. 68 PROMISE OF PARADISE by Karen Lawton Barrett
Gabriel is surprised to find that Eden's beauty is not just skin deep.

No. 69 OCEAN OF DREAMS by Patricia Hagan
Is Jenny just another shipboard romance to Officer Kirk Moen?

No. 70 SUNDAY KIND OF LOVE by Lois Faye Dyer
Trace literally sweeps beautiful, ebony-haired Lily off her feet.

Meteor Publishing Corporation
Dept. 492, P. O. Box 41820, Philadelphia, PA 19101-9828

Please send the books I've indicated below. Check or money order only—no cash, stamps or C.O.D.s (PA residents, add 6% sales tax). I am enclosing $2.95 plus 75¢ handling fee for *each* book ordered.

Total Amount Enclosed: $_____.

___ No. 47	___ No. 53	___ No. 59	___ No. 65
___ No. 48	___ No. 54	___ No. 60	___ No. 66
___ No. 49	___ No. 55	___ No. 61	___ No. 67
___ No. 50	___ No. 56	___ No. 62	___ No. 68
___ No. 51	___ No. 57	___ No. 63	___ No. 69
___ No. 52	___ No. 58	___ No. 64	___ No. 70

Please Print:
Name _____
Address _____ Apt. No. _____
City/State _____ Zip _____

Allow four to six weeks for delivery. Quantities limited.